THE DAY THE DONKEY DROPPED DEAD

THE DAY THE
DONKEY DROPPED DEAD

SAM HAY

CATNIP BOOKS
Published by Catnip Publishing Ltd
14 Greville Street
London EC1N 8SB

First published 2013
1 3 5 7 9 10 8 6 4 2

Text © 2013 Sam Hay
Illustrations © 2013 Tom Morgan-Jones

A CIP catalogue record for this book is available from the British Library

ISBN 978-1-84647-157-5

Printed in Poland

www.catnippublishing.co.uk

For Alice and Archie

Middle Spit Sands

Lower Spit
Lighthouse –
Several miles
down the coast

Car Park _ _ _

Mrs Hunter's
Hotel

Sea
Caves

Rocky Spit
of Land

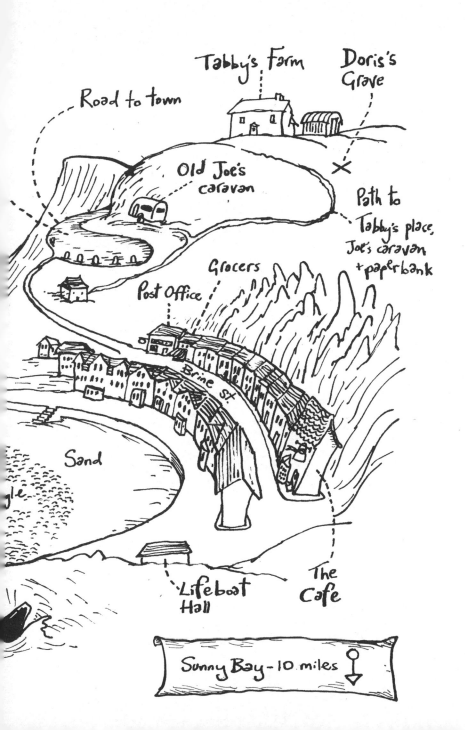

CHAPTER 1

When Doris the donkey dropped dead one damp morning in July, everyone said it was a sign. Doris had plodded her way up and down the beach for the best part of a century. Now, she lay, a dark hairy heap, tongue out, eyes glazed, the bells on her bridle still tinkling softly in the wind.

I'm ashamed to say I wasn't sorry. Doris was a bad-tempered beast at the best of times. She hated kids. She never missed an opportunity to nip or kick, and she left the beach looking like a currant bun, dotted with steamy brown dung. The only person who truly loved Doris was Old Joe, the donkey man. He stood over her now, shaking his head and sucking his false teeth.

'This will be the end of the town,' he croaked. 'You mark my words. It won't survive without Doris.'

Joe had a point. Middle Spit Sands was already on its last legs. It's a gloomy spot tucked high in the armpit of a gigantic length of rock spitting out into the sea. Even those who've been holidaying here for ever avoid it these days. And I don't blame them. It's not the sort of place I'd choose for a holiday. For starters, there's very little sun. There's not much sand either, just a small strip surrounded by dark shingle. And now the town's only donkey was dead.

I looked around as a small crowd gathered, hushed and solemn, giving Doris the respect she deserved. Doris may have been a bad-tempered old thing, but she was still a legend – she outlived all the other donkeys years ago. And although she'd stopped giving rides, she was always there, ambling along the beach, decorating it with dung.

Doris was the most famous face in town. She adorned every postcard. The gift shop sold plastic models of her. And she'd even had an ice cream named after her. If you pop into the Whistling Kettle café on Brine Street and ask for a 'Doris' you'll be given a double-chocolate superwhip with banana puffs on the side.

Old Joe sighed. 'We need to give her a proper send off, mind. Flowers. Music. The lot. Doris must be buried with full Middle Spit honours.'

Everyone nodded in agreement, as though a state funeral for a donkey was a perfectly reasonable request.

'I'll bring my bugle,' called out Annie Button. (Six foot three and built like a tank, Annie Button ran the post office and a guest house. And she was a champion bugle player to boot.)

'You can bury her on my land, Joe,' called Tabby.

(Thomas Toot, known as Tabby to his friends because his hair was stripy like a cat's, farmed the wind-thrashed land above our town. Against all odds, somehow he managed to keep alive a scrawny flock of sheep, two milking cows and some wild-looking chickens that were almost as scary as Doris!)

'And Davie and I will dig her grave.'

What?

I'm Davie, and that was my dad volunteering my gravedigging services! (Just for the record, my full name is Davie Hart, I'm nearly ten, and I live above the Whistling Kettle café, which my mum and dad bought last year.)

I gave him a look, one that I hoped said '*Hang on! I don't want to go and dig a grave for a bad-tempered donkey*' but obviously it didn't work, because he turned back to Tabby and started making arrangements to move 'the deceased'.

Less than an hour later, I was bumping along on the floor of Tabby's tractor trailer next to Doris while Old

Joe and the rest of the town went back to our café to have a 'Doris' and make preparations for the funeral.

'I don't see why we have to do it!' I grumbled, trying not to look at Doris's tongue, which was vibrating gently between her yellowed teeth as the tractor hauled us up the hill.

'Because that's what you do when you live somewhere like Middle Spit Sands,' said my dad in his patient voice. 'You help your neighbours, Davie.'

He had a point and I couldn't really grumble – the people who live here are okay in their weird, slightly scary, mad as cheese sort of a way. The problem was I didn't want to be *their* neighbour. I wanted to go back to our old neighbours. Back to our old house in our normal town, several hundred miles away from Middle Spit Sands, where people had normal names, and did normal things on Saturday mornings – like football or skateboarding or watching telly – instead of digging donkey graves . . . in the rain!

CHAPTER 2

'Come on, Davie – put your back into it!'

I gritted my teeth and heaved another load of earth out of the hole. Living in Middle Spit Sands wasn't supposed to be like this. When my parents had first mentioned the idea of moving to the seaside, it had seemed the most exciting thing in the world. What kid wouldn't want to spend every day on the beach? And on first viewing, Middle Spit Sands seemed to have a lot going for it.

For starters, there were the cliffs. They towered over the town, rough and jagged, as though they'd been hacked back from the sea by an angry Ninja giant. Birds nested there. Strange grasses sprouted from the rocks. And at night they seemed to glow green in the moonlight.

The town itself sat at the bottom of the cliffs, as if dumped there by the same Ninja giant. And although it wasn't much to look at, just a few rows of grey houses, it was right by the sea, which stretched out in front of it like an enormous black puddle. And when the tide was out, the beach was a crater of shingle and sand, strewn with massive boat-ripping rocks and slithery sea life.

The houses on the sea front were mostly small hotels and guest houses, with a few tourist shops in between. Behind, on Brine Street, were the grocer's and the post office. And at the far end of the row, right on the corner, was the Whistling Kettle café. My home.

To be honest it was in a bit of a state. Its shabby white-washed walls were peeling. Its blue window frames were rotten, and the front door didn't quite meet at the bottom so a wind constantly whistled underneath. Inside, the tables wobbled, the chairs were mouldy and the floor was the colour of sick. But it felt like a special place. Mostly because it had the best ice creams I'd ever tasted! It had all the usual flavours – chocolate, strawberry, vanilla – and some weird ones too – windberry, lemon bark, crackle gum, widdle grass, rock apple . . . and with them they made more than a hundred crazy combinations all served up in tall sundae glasses that sparkled when the light hit them.

The second I stuck my spoon into a Choc-chip Double-whip Flip, I was sunk. After that I made it my mission to try as many different ones as possible – from the Raging Volcano, which erupted with lemonade when you pierced the top, to the Strawberry Snow Bomb, which exploded on your spoon with little pieces of freeze-dried strawberries and space dust. And that was how Mum and Dad tricked me into moving to Middle Spit Sands.

We'd gone there on holiday. And it was day four of

our visit. I was halfway through a Hot Banana Topper Whopper when they told me that the café was up for sale and they'd like to buy it. They promised me an ice cream every day and, even better, a job in the café making the amazing sundaes. How could I refuse? It was an ice-cream dream come true and, like a mug, I bought it. But almost as soon as we arrived, I realised I'd made the biggest mistake of my life . . .

'Come on, Davie, stop daydreaming, they'll be here soon.'

There were three of us digging Doris's grave – Dad, me and Tabby Toot, though really Tabby was doing most of the work. He was like a human digger – never stopping, never breaking sweat. Whereas me and Dad were bright red and puffed out, like we'd been digging for days. Then suddenly we heard it – Annie Button's bugle, playing a long, low, mournful sound that echoed up the hillside like an army in retreat.

'They're coming,' said Tabby. 'Quick now, lads . . .'

He wiped the rain out of his eyes and stepped up the pace, shovelling earth like a mad machine. Dad and I did our bit as well. We'd just finished and were scrambling back out of the hole when everyone appeared. Mum was there too, helping Joe up the field and holding a bunch of flowers.

I've never been to a funeral before. But I've seen a few on telly. And I reckon this was a good one. The whole town was there – about twenty or so people – eyes lowered, heads bowed, pretending not to notice as the rain lashed their faces and the wind whipped their backs. They formed a solemn circle around the hole. Doris lay next to it, her coat drenched and those bridle bells still tinkling eerily in the wind.

Tabby offered to say a few words. And everyone stepped back to give him room. He leaned on his spade as he spoke, sweeping his soaking hair out of his eyes.

'We've all known Doris a long time,' he said, having to shout a bit over the noise of the wind. 'And we've all got our own special memories of her. Let's take a moment or two to think about what Doris meant to us . . .'

I tried hard to think kind thoughts, honestly I did. But all I could remember was her biting or kicking me, or blowing bottom wind in my face!

'She was a real character,' said Tabby, winking at me. 'And we'll never forget her.'

Then he stepped back. It was Joe's turn now . . .

The old man stood silently for a few minutes, buffeted by the wind, and then he said softly, 'Goodbye, old girl. I'll miss you.' He blew her a kiss and then turned to face the crowd and everyone held their breath.

Just so you know, Joe wasn't the friendliest bloke in the world. He had a sharp tongue and a stern face. According to Tabby, he'd had his heart broken as a teenager when his girlfriend ran off with a Punch and Judy man. Since then he'd devoted his life to his donkeys, and people always came second.

'Many of you have known me all your lives,' he said gruffly. 'You might think I'm old, but Doris was even older than me . . .' (I tried to do the maths, but it hurt my head.) '. . . Doris *was* our town,' Joe went on, 'and I know I've said this already – but I'll say it again – without her, I can't see a future for Middle Spit Sands.'

As he spoke there was a distant rumble of thunder and the sky turned black.

'We've had hard times here before,' said Joe, his

voice breaking a little with emotion. 'And we've survived, just about . . . but not now. Businesses are failing. Guests houses are closing. No one wants to come here on holiday any more.'

There was another rumble of thunder – closer now.

'Mark my words,' said Joe, wagging his wizened old finger at us. 'Doris's passing marks the end of Middle Spit Sands – the end of us all!'

And as if to underline the point, there was a sudden crack of lightning overhead, like a gunshot. I jumped. The others gasped. But Joe just nodded, as though the heavens had heard him and agreed. Then he took the flowers from Mum, laid them next to Doris, and shuffled off into the rain.

No one seemed to know what to do next, so Annie Button took up her bugle and started playing 'The Last Post'. The crowd began to move away. And I was hoping I could go too. I longed for some dry clothes and a mug of steaming hot chocolate in our café. But I'd forgotten that Doris wasn't actually buried yet. And as Dad handed me my shovel, I realised my hot chocolate would have to wait.

Have you ever buried a dead donkey? It's hard.

For starters, they're enormous! And stiff. And they stick out in all sorts of places. Soaking-wet dead donkeys are even worse – they weigh a ton. But luckily Tabby knew what to do. He and Dad threaded ropes underneath Doris. Then the three of us grasped the ends. And slipping and sliding in the mud we somehow managed to lower Doris into the pit.

As I shovelled earth on top of her, I winced in pain – I had blisters on the palms of my hands from digging, my arms ached, my back hurt. I was soaking wet and numb with cold. I looked up at the black sky above and shook my head. There was no doubt about it, Doris was definitely having the last laugh – and the joke was on me. Ice-cream dreams or not, life in Middle Spit Sands was rubbish. Totally!

CHAPTER 3

I should probably tell you a bit more about myself. I'm small and skinny with dark brown hair. And if I had to, I reckon I could eat my weight in ice cream. Really. I love it! I'm also mad keen on skateboarding. And snowboarding! Not that there are many places to ride around here . . . but just to prove I can, I'll show you a picture:

That's me – the one with the black T-shirt and the big board. The tall boy is my cousin Vincent (he used to like boards too, before he became a pickled-onion munching Goth. Weird!) And that's Dad at the back making funny faces. He's like that, my dad, always laughing and joking. Mum's fun too, when she's not telling me off. But she's not in the picture. She refuses to have her photo taken. Here's another one:

It was taken the day we moved into the Whistling Kettle café. And that's Dad frying up his first cooked breakfast. He looks really excited, doesn't he? You see, the café was his dream come true. He used to be a plumber. But he always wanted to be a chef. Then one day he got so brassed off with blocked bogs that he started looking for a café to run instead. Which is how we ended up here. But it looked like Dad's dream job was turning into a nightmare . . .

You see business was bad in Middle Spit Sands. The number of visitors had been falling every year, and by the time we bought the café, loads of shops and guest houses had closed. Our first months here were hard. Few people came in the winter. And even the spring and summer months, which should have been our busiest time, were quiet. And now that Doris was dead, who knew what was going to happen!

After the funeral it didn't stop raining for a week, and the last of the visitors who were around packed up early and left. It seemed Old Joe's prophecy of doom was coming true. I wasn't too worried about it though, apart from the fact I was bored out of my brain. Other than going to the beach, there's not much to do around here. I mean, I love looking for crabs and shells and stuff, but there are only so many days you can go rock pooling in the rain. There are no parks. No cinema. Not even any other kids to hang out with. That was the worst bit. No mates! None of my friends from school live near by. (Just so you know, my school's in a place called Sunny Bay, ten miles up the coast.) So most of the time, I just pottered about in the kitchen, teaching myself how to make ice-cream sundaes. Luckily I had the café's cookbook to help me. It was amazing, like a book of magic spells – big and brown and smelling of strawberries. Not that I got much chance to show off my ice-cream sundae making skills . . . until, that is, one damp afternoon when life took an unexpected (and unwelcome) turn.

I was in the kitchen washing up cups and saucers (whenever the sundae business is slow, I'm demoted to dish washer), when suddenly I heard my parents' voices in the café. For the last hour or so they'd been working through the accounts (and bills), but now they were talking, and from the tone of Mum's voice, I knew things were bad.

'It just won't work, Michael,' she said, closing the book with a thud. 'There's no way we'll survive another winter. We've got bills coming out of our ears and nothing to pay them with.'

I stopped washing up and stood stock-still.

'We need to face facts,' said Mum desperately. 'We rushed into this without knowing anything about running a café, and it shows. We're nearly broke. If things don't improve soon, we'll have to think about selling up.'

I was so shocked I couldn't move. Selling up? I'm ashamed to say, a sudden wave of excitement washed over me. Maybe we'd move back to our old town! I strained to hear Dad's reply . . . but it never came, because just then the café door opened and the conversation ended abruptly. Then . . .

'Davie!' It was Dad's voice, much more cheerful now. 'Come here – you've got a customer.'

I ditched the dishes and trotted through, my pencil and pad at the ready. Then my heart sank. A small girl with hair the colour of cherries sat there grinning at me. I looked around hoping she'd brought six hungry big brothers with her, or even just a set of parents or grandparents . . . but there was no one else.

'Yes?' I said wearily. After all, it didn't look like I

was going to get much of a chance to make one of my biggest and best creations. She probably only wanted a glass of tap water – a small one!

'Hello,' she grinned, 'I'm Ruby. Aunt Annie told me there was a new kid in town. So I thought I'd come and say hi.'

I blinked at her. Aunt Annie. *Who was she?* I wracked my brain. (It didn't take long.) And then the penny dropped. She must mean Annie Button from the post office.

'I was born here, you know . . .' she beamed.

'That's nice,' I said, trying to look enthusiastic.

'But we moved away for a few years – touring, you know . . .'

'Er, yeah,' I said, not sure what she was on about.

'But now we're moving back. So you and me can be pals.'

She grinned at me, as though this was the best news in the world. It wasn't. It definitely wasn't! I gritted my teeth. This was just my luck. A kid in town at last – and she was a girl. This grinning, silly, ridiculous girl.

'Did you want to order something?' I said changing the subject.

She glanced at the menu. 'Er . . . okay – I'll have a Sea Swamp, please, with extra crackle berries, and three wafers but no waffles. Oh, and don't forget the mermaid cream.'

I was so shocked. I just stood there with my mouth open.

'You do know how to make a Sea Swamp, don't you?' Her face was suddenly serious. 'Only, I've been eating them since I was a baby, so I could show you, if you don't.'

'Of course I do!' I snapped. (Though of course, I didn't. I hadn't even heard of a Sea Swamp before).

Her eyes twinkled mischievously. 'Great, then I can't wait to try it.'

I stalked back to the kitchen muttering under my breath. Why couldn't she have asked for an Orange Fizz or a Lemon Wuzzle – or even a Doris? I'd practised them. I heaved open the café cookbook, hoping to find the recipe for a Sea Swamp – the book wasn't in alphabetical order. I leafed through one way, and then the other, but I couldn't see the recipe anywhere. I checked again, faster this time. I had to hurry up. After all, she was a customer. And there weren't many of them knocking about in Middle Spit Sands.

'It's near the back!'

I jumped. I'd been so engrossed in what I was doing I hadn't spotted Ruby coming through to the kitchen.

'Want me to show you?' she grinned.

'No!' I said crossly. 'You're not even supposed to be here. It's staff only.'

'Don't be silly,' she said, her face reddening. 'We're the only two kids in this town. We might as well be friends. I mean, we can't exactly avoid each other.'

I frowned. And tried to think of some reason why I was too busy to be her friend. But just then her small hand shot out and she pointed at a small recipe halfway down one page.

'There!' she said triumphantly. 'Sea Swamp sundae. All you need now is the recipe for Mermaid cream,' she giggled. And I had to resist the urge to clobber her with the cookbook.

CHAPTER 4

It turned out that a Sea Swamp was actually very easy to make. And I certainly didn't need Ruby's help. But it seemed more trouble to try and get rid of her. She never stopped talking.

She told me her full name was Ruby Violet Button and her dad was Annie Button's brother. (As well as the post office, Annie kept a small guest house just three doors down from the café, where Ruby and her mum were staying. So now we were neighbours too. Grrrrr!) She said she was ten years old (her birthday was in June so she was three months older than me! Double Grrrrr!) And her dad was the drummer in a heavy metal band. Apparently she and her mum had been touring with him for the last three years (Ruby had been home-schooled in the back of the tour bus) but now she and her mum were moving back to Middle Spit Sands so Ruby would be settled when she started secondary school next year.

I didn't know whether to believe her or not. But I couldn't be bothered arguing. By then, I was too busy searching through the giant freezers at the back of the kitchen to find all the ingredients I needed for her silly Sea Swamp sundae.

If you ever want to make one, it consists of mint choc chip, chocolate fudge and pistachio ice cream piled up nice and tall with swirls of green apple and chocolate sauce swished around the top. I found the wafers for her, but said we'd run out of Mermaid cream. (A total fib.) Then she made me sit next to her while she ate it.

By now, we were on our own in the café. Mum and Dad had retreated upstairs with calls of, 'Shout if it gets busy.' (If only.) We sat in silence for a bit and I listened to the wind whistling under the door, the windows rattling in reply.

'I see it's raining again,' said Ruby, licking green sludge off her spoon. 'Aunt Annie says this has been the worst summer ever – and that's saying something.'

'Bet you're gutted to be moving back here,' I said gloomily.

Ruby frowned. 'No, I love it. I've spent every summer in Middle Spit Sands since we started touring. It's better than being stuck on a boring bus all day.'

I grimaced. 'But nothing ever happens and there's nothing to do.'

'You need a few hobbies,' said Ruby cheerfully. 'I collect things – fossils, rocks, bird bones . . .' (I made a barf face, but she pretended not to notice.) 'And the caves around the point are brilliant. Me and Dad explored them once. And if you walk along the coast path for a mile or so, there's an amazing old lighthouse . . .'

I sighed and kicked aimlessly at a piece of lino that had come unstuck on the floor under the table. 'Yeah, yeah, but it's so quiet! Living here is a bit like having your head stuck in a sleeping bag. And it's been raining for weeks. Mind you, I might be moving soon. Mum says if business doesn't get any better, we'll have to sell up and leave.'

'Really?' Ruby cocked her head to one side like a budgie. 'That's a shame.'

I shrugged. 'Not really. I'd be happy to go.'

Ruby's face hardened. 'It's not that bad.'

'Yes, it is,' I scowled. 'No one in their right mind would come to live in Middle Spit Sands!' I didn't mean to be quite so rude but for some reason Ruby's cheerfulness made me feel even more fed up than usual.

But she wasn't cheerful now. Her face turned purple. 'Maybe you just don't belong here. You certainly don't deserve the Whistling Kettle café. The sooner you clear off the better!' Then she dug around in her jeans for some coins, flung them on the table and flounced out, her cherry pigtails bobbing crossly.

Good riddance, I thought. But unfortunately that wasn't the last I saw of Ruby Button.

You know how it is. When you're trying to avoid someone they pop up everywhere. For the next couple of weeks I was plagued by Ruby. She was in the post office when I went to buy stamps. She was in the grocer's when I went in for apples. And she invaded the beach all the time too – kite flying, bird watching or just digging up stuff from the shingle. (Things for her 'collections' I presumed.)

Meanwhile, things at home got worse. Mum called an estate agent – a slimy sort named Roger Pilkington-Smith, who came down from Sunny Bay to talk about selling the café. I didn't like the look of him. He was barrel-chested – a beef-steak of a man with small eyes and big hair. He looked around our place, huffing and puffing and making notes on his hand-held computer. When he'd finished he sighed and said we wouldn't get much for it.

Dad didn't listen. He was pouring over business books he'd borrowed from the library which all had silly titles like: *How to Manage Your Way Out of a Mess* and *Bounce Your Business Back from the Brink!*

As a result he came up with lots of ideas to save the café. There were half-price Tuesdays and Thursdays. Buy one get one free on bacon sarnies. And three for two on doughnuts. But it was no good. There were no tourists to take up the offers. 'For Sale' signs started to appear around town. Then some of the remaining shops closed. And even the grocer – Mr Blair – talked about retiring. It seemed like I was the only person in Middle Spit Sands who wasn't utterly miserable. Until the day I found my dad crying.

CHAPTER 5

It should be a rule really; a law maybe. Parents must not (not ever!) cry in front of their kids. Because it rips you up. Really it does. It's like having a teaspoon stabbed in your heart two hundred times a day.

It was a Tuesday afternoon, three weeks after Ruby arrived. I'd been mooching around the far end of the beach, but when the rain got too heavy I headed home. And that's when I found Dad, standing outside the café in the rain, without his coat. He was peering up at a big sign that had appeared above the café door:

BUSINESS FOR SALE
For more details contact
PILKINGTON-SMITH PROPERTIES
of Sunny Bay

His face was white. There were dark shadows under his eyes, and he wore an expression of such despair that I could hardly look at him.

'What are you doing out here, Dad?' I asked, trying to sound jolly. 'Come inside, you'll catch a cold.'

But he didn't hear me. 'Do you know something, Davie,' he said, pointing at the sign. 'I wasn't a great plumber and now I'm an even worse café owner. This was my dream, and now it's over.' He sniffed a bit, and then he turned to face me. 'I'm sorry, son, for dragging you here, away from your friends . . . and now it looks like I'll be dragging you off somewhere else . . .'

And then I saw them – tears, *real* tears – only a couple, mind you, hardly noticeable really but enough to floor me. My dad was crying. My dad, the big silly bloke who could fix anything – taps, toilets, tiramisu – and here he was, in bits. He seemed to be shrinking before me, his face becoming old and defeated-looking. And suddenly my whole world began to wobble. I felt a knot in my stomach. My throat was dry. And then a new, even worse feeling flooded my blood – guilt. It washed over me in a huge miserable wave. This was my fault. It was me who had wanted to leave Middle Spit

Sands. It was me who moaned constantly about the town. And it was me who wanted Dad's business to fail so we could go home. Somehow I had willed this to happen. And now I felt terrible. 'Don't worry, Dad,' I said hoarsely. 'Something will turn up. We might not have to sell the café . . . maybe we can make it work.'

I looked at Dad, and then at the café – its cheery lights glowing in the gloom – and suddenly I felt a bit sad too. I tried to imagine never seeing it again. Never making another ice-cream sundae . . . and I realised with a bump that maybe I didn't want to leave Middle Spit Sands as much as I thought I did. Seeing the 'For Sale' sign above the door was a shock. My ice-cream dream was about to end. And I wasn't sure I really wanted it to. Not yet. But more than anything I just wanted to see Dad smile again.

As we went inside, trailing wet footprints across the sick-coloured floor, and I smelt the mould and saw the shiny sundae glasses stacked on the counter, I realised this was home. It was my dad's dream, and because of that it was where we belonged. And somehow I had to make sure we stayed so Dad had a chance to make it work.

But how? I thought of nothing else for the rest of the day. From somewhere I had to find a load of tourists. And fast!

But from where? I wracked my brains while I got on with my chores. I washed the cups, I put out the bins. I scrubbed all the tables, and still I couldn't come up with anything. Eventually, when I ran out of stuff to do inside, I gathered up the old newspapers and headed out into the rain to take them to the paper bank. It was halfway up the hill on the way out of town; a steep hike on a good day and not something I would normally do. But today was different. I needed to get out; to keep busy. For some reason it helped me to think. Even so, it wasn't a pleasant climb. The wind was blowing straight into my face. It was cold and, worse still, I could see Ruby in the distance, her arms full of newspapers, obviously heading for the same place.

Of course she got there first. She was built like a small goat. And when I finally puffed my way up there, she gave me a dirty look. I ignored her. I wasn't in the mood for a fight. I had bigger problems to contend with than Ruby Violet Button.

As usual the paper bank was overflowing (even the

bin men had long forgotten Middle Spit Sands). I put down my bags anyway, next to the paper bank, along with a dozen or so others, but just as I did, a sudden gust of wind blew straight in off the sea, sending sheets of newspaper whooshing wildly up into the air.

For one crazy minute me and Ruby looked like we were in one of those toy snowstorms, surrounded by fluttering sheets of paper. We both made a grab for them, but, then . . . CLUNK! We bashed heads. For a second we squared up to each other, ready for a row, and then I grinned. I just couldn't help myself. And Ruby smiled too. And suddenly we were both racing and chasing up and down the path, trying to catch all the paper. It wasn't easy. Just as you got close to one, it took off again. But eventually we got them all, and stuffed them back into the bags. It was then I spotted a single sheet that was still free – dancing around on the ground. I made a leap and landed on it.

'Got you!' I shouted. And Ruby gave me a cheer. I went to stuff it in a bag, when something made me glance down. I still don't know why I took a closer look. But it's just as well I did, because that glance probably saved our town . . . it probably saved us all.

CHAPTER 6

I looked at the paper briefly, then I did a double-take. It was the oddest newspaper I'd ever seen; the page was a sickly yellow colour and looked very oldy worldy. All the stories were crammed tightly together, printed in heavy black type, like the cookbook in our café. There were no photographs, and around the edge of the page was a thin black border, as though it was announcing the death of some great king or queen. At the top I read its title – the *Darkington Times*. I glanced at the headlines and frowned. They were decidedly odd too:

SPECTACULAR SPOOKING SCARES SIXTY SCOUTS JAMBOREE CANCELLED

HEADLESS HARRY RETURNS!

GREY LADY TO RETIRE

BLOOD-SOAKED BRIDE VOWS TO WED AGAIN

Each story sounded more strange and spooky than the last. Then something really caught my eye – *Great Wet Getaways! Avoid the last of the summer sun in these deliciously dark and dingy destinations* – it went on to list five 'great' places for a wet holiday, where heavy rain and howling winds were guaranteed. And then underneath the article I spotted something that made my heart stop.

'Ruby!' I squeaked. 'Look at this . . .'

She peered over my arm. 'What?'

'They're adverts. Adverts for really horrible places to go on holiday. Look!'

'Hangman's Cottage,' read Ruby. 'Dinner, bed and breakfast. Rats, bats and black cats welcome.'

'And this one,' I said, pointing excitedly to another.

'Crow Castle – dark, dingy dungeon to rent . . . cauldron facilities on request.'

'And that one . . .'

'Goblin Hole for hire – hot and cold running slime . . .' Ruby giggled.

'And here's another,' I said. 'A horrible welcome awaits at Hellington Hall. Fantastically foul food from top kitchen witch Ethel Flugg.'

'Kitchen witch?' said Ruby. 'That's ridiculous.'

'But don't you see,' I said excitedly. 'It doesn't matter whether it's ridiculous or not . . . what matters is that there are obviously people out there – people who read this crazy paper – who want to go on holiday to horrible places. People who love rain and wind and black clouds . . . strange people who like to sleep in dungeons and dress up like witches . . .'

'Or goblins,' added Ruby.

'Or goblins . . . But it doesn't matter how mad they are – our town needs them! Think about it, Ruby – our town is more horrible than any of these places. All we have to do is write our own advert, tell them how bad it is, and they'll flock to Middle Spit Sands!'

'But you hate it here,' said Ruby, her face turning hard again. 'What do you care if they come or not?'

'I do care,' I said quietly, 'because my dad wants to stay here. And . . . well, so do I, for now. I'm sorry about before. But this is our chance to save this town, and you've got to help.'

Ruby didn't look convinced, but she followed me back to the café anyway. Meanwhile my head was bursting with ideas. It felt like I was on to something. Could this crazy paper be the solution to all our problems? It was worth a try. And I wanted to get started straight away. I was planning to write the biggest, best advert ever – and send it off to the *Darkington Times* that night. But before I did, I decided to make a final peace offering to Ruby – a special ice-cream sundae. And to get us in a spooky mood I called it the Haunted House! It had three scoops of vanilla ice cream, one of mint choc chip, a squirt of blood (strawberry sauce) and a bloody eyeball on top (well, actually a cherry on a cocktail stick). The sight of it seemed to cheer Ruby up, and as we tucked into our sundaes we had another look at the *Darkington Times* . . .

It was certainly a weird sheet of newspaper. The main story – *Headless Harry Returns!* – was all about some mad knight named Harold de Bon Ville, who was now back in the saddle, haunting the back roads of Bedfordshire, after rediscovering his lost head, which he'd found hidden in a museum in Kent. It was all completely bonkers, of course . . . and yet strangely it didn't read like a joke.

'You know, Ruby, we'll need to make our advert super scary,' I said, plunging my spoon into my ice cream, 'because the people who read this paper obviously take their ghost stories very seriously.'

'But do we really want crazy people to come here?' said Ruby. 'I know we're desperate but . . .'

'Maybe they're not crazy,' I said. 'At least not all the time. My cousin Vincent likes wearing dark clothes and listening to spooky music, and he's pretty straight. It's probably just a hobby. You know, like some people dress up as Vikings at the weekend and charge about the fields bashing each other on the head, but during the week they're perfectly normal people. It's like play-acting for grown-ups. The people who read this paper are probably just the same.'

'Mmm,' said Ruby. 'Weekend weirdoes? Maybe . . .'

I pushed away the empty sundae glass and picked up my pen. 'How about this?' I said. 'Come to Middle Spit Sands for bad weather and gruesome grub. Rats, bats and pointy black hats welcome . . .'

'Mmm,' said Ruby. 'Not bad.'

'Okay, how about this then: Come to Middle Spit Sands for a frightfully bad time – rain and wind guaranteed!'

'Maybe . . .' Ruby tapped her teeth (rather annoyingly) with her spoon for a few moments, and then her eyes lit up. 'I know! What about changing our town's name, so it sounds spookier?' She made a grab for the pen and scribbled furiously for a bit then spun the paper to face me. 'What do you think?'

I read it once, and then again. It was good. Very good. So good I felt a bit peeved that I hadn't written it myself. But I was feeling generous. 'Perfect!' I said sincerely. 'Write it out neatly and I'll fetch an envelope.'

This is what she'd written:

Come to Screaming Sands,
the ghastliest ghost town in the world.
Howling gales and torrential
rain guaranteed.
Dark caves, spooky attics and horribly
haunted houses available for hire.
For bookings contact Davie Hart at
the Poisoned Kettle café,
Brine Street, Screaming Sands
(near Middle Spit Sands).

Screaming Sands! I loved it. It sounded deliciously dark. And the Poisoned Kettle café fitted perfectly too.

I searched the *Darkington Times* for an address and found one, written in small print at the bottom of the sheet. I wrote the envelope myself. But as I looked at it, I felt something was missing. And it wasn't just the stamp. The envelope needed a final grisly touch; something that would make it look seriously spooky.

'Blood!' I said.

'What?' Ruby cocked her head to one side again, like a confused budgie. (It was actually one of her most annoying habits, even worse than the teeth tapping.)

I frowned. 'We should dribble some real blood on the envelope, so they know we mean business. Come on . . .' Without thinking I jabbed the cocktail stick from my ice cream straight into the end of my thumb. A tiny bud of blood immediately appeared. Boy, did it hurt! But I gritted my teeth – I didn't want to be a sap in front of Ruby. Reluctantly, she did the same. And with our fingers still throbbing we smeared a thin trace of blood on the front of the envelope.

'It looks like a tea stain,' grumbled Ruby.

She was right, of course. It didn't look remotely spooky. But there was no time to redo it because just then I heard Dad on the stairs, and I didn't want to tell him what we were up to – not yet. So, gathering up the newspaper, I quickly hustled Ruby out of the door, crumpling the envelope into her pocket. 'Don't forget to post it as soon as you can,' I whispered.

And the deed was done. All we could do now was wait, and pray that a few of the 'lets pretend' weekend weirdoes would book a holiday soon. I just hoped it would be in time to save the town. But events moved faster than we could have imagined . . . Inhumanely fast.

CHAPTER 7

It was the following day, another wet afternoon. I was in the kitchen trying out a new ice-cream recipe when it happened. As usual, there was a cold wind blowing hard off the sea, but I was snug and warm in the kitchen – it's one of the few places that's always cosy. Just as I was reaching for a pot of sugar sprinkles, one of the windows suddenly flew open, letting in a blast of icy cold wind. I was so shocked I dropped the pot, spilling millions of sprinkles all over the floor.

'Pants!' I said crossly, reaching to close the window.

But I couldn't do it. The wind was so strong it pushed me right back, hard against the wall, pinning me there. I was too shocked to scream. Meanwhile the sprinkles on the floor began to dance wildly around, like crazy multi-coloured ants. Then they stopped dancing and started to form patterns. No, not patterns – words! And then a message began to form . . .

WOULD LIKE TO BOOK ROOM WITH A VIEW. It said. *WILL ARRIVE NEXT FULL MOON. SINCERLEY YOURS, AGATHA GUM*.

'Blimey!' I gasped. And then just as suddenly, the wind changed direction and was violently sucked out of the window, which snapped shut loudly behind it, and I was free to move again.

I stared open-mouthed for a moment, and then recovered enough to bend down to take a closer look at the message. 'Hell's teeth!' I gasped. What could it mean? And who was Agatha Gum? But just then there was the sound of footsteps and . . .

'Davie? What are you doing down there?'

I looked up to find Mum at the door, hands on her hips, looking cross. 'What a mess,' she said. 'Come on now – help me clear this up.'

'But, Mum,' I gasped. 'It's a message . . . look.'

She looked, and so did I. But there was no message now – just a huge, messy pile of sprinkles.

Mum frowned. 'Come on – stop playing with food. It's nearly teatime.'

I didn't argue. I was too busy wondering whether I was losing my mind.

If I was, it was happening fast. And by bedtime, there would be none left at all, because the next incident happened barely twenty minutes later.

I was sitting in the café eating my tea. It was soup. Green soup. Not my favourite. And to be honest I was dawdling; stirring it one way, and then the other.

'What?' I said to Mum as she gave me a hard look across the table. 'I'm just letting it cool down.'

'If it gets any cooler, a penguin will pop up and pinch it!' Mum shook her head and started telling Dad a very dull story about the price of carrots. He looked about as interested as I was. And he didn't seem to want his soup either. He was staring out the window, watching the darkness descend. (The days were always short in Middle Spit Sands – whatever the season.)

Meanwhile, I was still mulling over the sprinkles incident. Had it really happened, or had I imagined it? Then, as I stared blankly into my soup, I noticed some small circles appearing in the centre like tiny smoke rings. They were spiralling slowly outwards, getting bigger with every turn – it was quite hypnotic. Then my eyes nearly popped out. The circles were turning into words, spiralling around the edge of my bowl.

BOOK ME A CAVE. COLD, DARK AND DINGY . . . ARRIVING NEXT FULL MOON. FOND REGARDS, DARKLY SAGE, ESQUIRE

'Mum! Dad!' I squawked. 'Look!'

But of course there was nothing to see. As soon as I looked up, the message vanished. And all my parents saw was me pointing at my (untouched) bowl of soup. Needless to say, Mum didn't see the funny side, especially as I wouldn't eat the soup (I was far too shocked, and by then it was cold), so I got sent upstairs for a bath and an early bed. I didn't mind too much. I needed to think. Agatha Gum? Darkly Sage? Even if I was going doo-lally, where was I dreaming up such weird names from?

I turned on the hot tap in the bathroom, and waited while the bath filled up. I like the bathroom. It's rather an odd colour – aubergine, according to Mum, which is a fairly frightful purple. But it's big and peaceful with a bath you could get lost in.

As I started to undress something on the mirror caught my eye. I grinned. Dad must have drawn one of his doodles. (Before we moved to Middle Spit Sands, he'd do that sometimes – draw a funny picture in the steam on the mirror, after his shower.) But as I peered a bit closer, I realised this was not my dad's work. It was a horribly life-like skull, with gaping mouth and empty eyes. And then a terrible thing happened. It moved! Really it did. Its eyes went all boggly and the mouth opened and a voice came out. To be honest, it wasn't actually a very scary voice, though seeing as it was coming from a talking steamy skull, drawn on my mirror, it was definitely enough to freak me out . . .

SORRY TO BE A BOTHER, BUT I'D JUST LIKE TO BOOK AN ATTIC ROOM. JACK SNOW IS THE NAME. I'LL BE ARRIVING WHEN THE MOON IS FULL. CHEERIOOOOO!

And then it vanished, leaving me a small sweaty heap of shock and surprise, cowering in the corner of our aubergine bathroom.

CHAPTER 8

Talking skulls! Messages in my soup bowl! Not to mention the freaky incident in the kitchen. I'd had enough. I abandoned my bath and raced back to my bedroom, closing the door tightly behind me. I was spooked! Utterly terrified. But before I could think what to do next, there was a sudden thud on the roof above me, as though something heavy had landed on it. Then the thud turned into a rumble as whatever it was began to roll across the roof until it reached the chimney, then . . . ROOOOOARRRR! It thundered down, crashing out of the fireplace straight into my room.

'AHHH!' I squeaked, diving for the bed. The thing was a massive ball of . . . 'Spiders!' I yelped, flattening my back against the wall. I watched in horror as thousands of them scuttled across the floor, fanning out like a big black wave.

'Mum! Dad!' I screamed. (I hate spiders!)

But they weren't actually after me – they had a job to do . . . and suddenly I realised what it was – another message. This one laid out on the carpet in front of me, spelled out in spiders:

THREE NORTH-FACING ROOMS FOR NEXT FULL MOON, wrote the spiders *FROM THE O'HARA SISTERS OF BALLYTWEDDLE. P.S. WE HATE PINK!*

As soon as I'd read the message the spiders rolled back into their ball and then instantly turned to dust.

'What on earth is going on?' Dad burst into the room, finding me standing on my bed with my eyes like pies, looking down at a big pile of dirt on the carpet.

'A soot ball,' grimaced Dad with a sigh. He peered up the chimney and shook his head. 'It obviously needs a good sweep. Not sure we can afford to do it right now, but I'll fetch some newspapers to block it up.'

Newspapers! There weren't any. I'd already taken them to the paper bank. It was just the excuse I needed. Before Dad could argue I pulled on my jumper and grabbed my boots. 'I recycled them all,' I explained. 'But Ruby might have some – I'll go and borrow a few.' Then I headed for the door (lifting the *Darkington Times* from my desk as I went past).

'But, Davie,' called Dad. 'It's late. It's getting dark out there . . . you hate the dark!'

The dark? Ha! As if that would spook me now! 'Back soon, Dad,' I yelled, as I raced down the stairs, two at a time. I had to talk to Ruby, tell her what was happening. But as I stepped outside the café door, I tripped over a giant black cat that was sitting on the doorstep and landed splat on the ground. As I staggered to my feet, the cat flashed its green eyes crossly at me and then spoke:

MISTRESS GREEN REQUESTS A ROOM WITH SPACE FOR HER CAT AND THREE PET RATS. SHE LIKES MIDNIGHT TREATS BUT WON'T EAT MEAT. SHE'S A STRICT VEGETARIAN!

I was so shocked I just stood there gawping at the cat. It looked back at me as if I was stupid. Then, obviously thinking I hadn't been listening properly, it repeated the message again, before vanishing off into the night. A talking cat? Whatever next? I felt my knees go weak, my legs wobble and my heart pound against my chest. In short, I was suddenly struck down by a major attack of the willies. Something super spooky was happening right here and now. Head down, I ran like the wind to Ruby's house.

She saw I was shaken as soon as she opened the door. Without waiting for an explanation she bundled me past her mum and her aunt, who were watching telly in the living room, and took me into their back kitchen where she made me a huge mug of hot chocolate.

And then it all came pouring out. As I spoke, Ruby's eyes widened, and widened. And widened even more, until she began to look like one of those weird bush-baby monkey things. When finally I ran out of breath, Ruby's eyes went back to normal.

'So you're telling me it worked?' she said with a frown. 'That we've got a bunch of crazies coming? But that's impossible because I never posted the letter.'

'What?'

'I lost it.' She shrugged. 'I'm sorry, Davie – it vanished on my way home from your house last night. There was a terrible mist. I retraced my steps this morning, but I couldn't find it.'

'But if you didn't post the letter, how can these oddballs even know about us?'

Ruby cocked her head. (That dreaded 'dead budgie' look again.) Then a light seemed to go on in her eyes. 'Have you still got the newspaper?'

I handed it over, and as she smoothed it out, I saw it straight away.

'There!' I shouted. Our advert was now on the back page. Somehow, without us even posting the letter, our advert had made it into the newspaper.

'But how can that be?' I gasped. 'How can a newspaper just change like that? And anyway – you lost the letter . . .'

'Because we're not dealing with a bunch of teachers and nurses who like to dress up at weekends,' said Ruby, her face chalk-white. 'These creatures – and their nutty newspaper – must be for real, Davie . . . Witches, ghosts, goblins . . .'

'Talking cats,' I added.

'Yep, and in three days time they'll all be here, on our doorstep.'

'Three days?' I squeaked.

'Yes,' said Ruby. 'I study the skies, Davie – it's one of my hobbies – and I know the next full moon is in three days' time.'

'Blimey,' I breathed. 'What are we going to do?'

Ruby tapped her teeth with her hot-chocolate spoon.

'Call a meeting,' she said solemnly. 'We'll make some leaflets telling everyone to come to a meeting and then we'll tell the whole town what we've done.'

'But they'll never believe us.' Why would they? *I* still didn't believe us.

Ruby shrugged. 'They'll have to, Davie. Because this is really happening.'

I gulped, and I felt a wave of excitement and anxiety rush through my belly.

But Ruby was grinning mischievously. 'We've done it, Davie ! We've saved the town!'

I just hoped she was right.

CHAPTER 9

Ruby appeared before breakfast. Luckily Mum and Dad were too busy worrying about the business to take much notice, so I made us both a breakfast sundae (ice cream and Shreddies), and we settled down in the café to work on the leaflets and posters.

EMERGENCY MEETING:
YOUR TOWN NEEDS YOU!
VILLAGE HALL, 11am TODAY

Ruby couldn't sit still. She was jiggling about in her chair and tapping her teeth excitedly with the end of her pen. I wasn't quite so lively. My head was fuzzy and I couldn't concentrate. You see, I hadn't slept a wink. As soon as I'd got back to the café, more messages had arrived. Some came quite politely, as though they'd been delivered by kind fairies – one was wrapped neatly round my toothbrush, another placed under my pillow, a third appeared in the soapy bubbles as I washed my face for bed. But others were much worse – an upended Lego box, with the message manically built up in bricks, before crashing back to nothing. A loud scary voice shouted up at me from the depths of the toilet when I went for a wee. And a really horrible one popped out of the plug hole as I brushed my teeth – it was a disgustingly slimy sheet of rolled-up paper covered in grot and grime. YUCK! I was glad to climb into bed that night, but just as I did another message arrived courtesy of a grumpy bat that fluttered down the chimney and squeaked a lot, before escaping through the window.

Each message vanished the minute I'd read it. So I wrote them down in a notebook that Ruby had given me for the job. Otherwise, she'd said, we'll forget who wants what and we'll get overbooked! I didn't like to admit it, but Ruby was annoyingly well organised.

'Come on, slow boots!' she called as we headed out to deliver the notes. By the time I caught up with her, she was already waiting by the gate at the bottom of

Tabby's field. 'I'll carry on up to Old Joe's caravan,' she said. 'And I'll do Mr Blair's shop too. Meet you back at the hall just before the meeting. Okay?'

'What if no one comes?'

'Of course they will,' she grinned. 'There's nothing else to do on a wet Wednesday in Middle Spit Sands.'

And she was right, of course. I walked through Tabby's gate and wound my way up through his field, past Doris's grave. I tried not to look at the mound of earth as I passed by; there was still something quite creepy about it. But as I drew level, I heard a terrifying sound – bells! Tiny bells, tinkling softly in the breeze. I gritted my teeth and told myself not to be so silly, it was probably just the wind (though a part of me wondered whether Doris was haunting me too, as payback for all my mean thoughts about her).

'Hello, Davie! You're out early.' It was Tabby.

I waved, glad to see his reassuring face at the top of the field. He was out feeding his chickens, and despite the rain was still wearing his usual khaki shorts and T-shirt. It always amazed me that Tabby didn't feel the cold like the rest of us.

'How are your mum and dad doing?' he asked.

I shrugged. 'Not so good. The café is up for sale,'

'I'd heard that.' Tabby sighed. 'Such a shame.' Then he smiled again. 'But maybe something will crop up. You never know, Davie, you need to look on the bright side.'

He took the leaflet I held out to him. 'An emergency meeting?' he raised his bushy eyebrows. 'Sounds intriguing.'

I nodded. 'Me and Ruby have a plan to help rescue Middle Spit Sands.'

Tabby didn't push me for details. 'Great stuff, Davie. I'll be there.'

And he was. They all were. The whole town turned out, just like Ruby had predicted. And as I sat at the front of the hall watching them take their seats, my palms turned sweaty and I started to get nervous.

Ruby wasn't. She was loving it; the drama, the excitement – the secret about to be revealed. She showed people to their seats, batting their questions aside, promising a full explanation soon, while I just sat in my chair biting my lip and trying not to catch anyone's eye.

It was a small hall with a tin roof and rattling

windows. It stood alone at the far end of the town, right on the sea front. Years ago, they'd kept the lifeboat in it. But that was when Middle Spit Sands was busier. Eventually they'd built a new life-boat station further up the coast, and since then the hall had lain empty. But it wasn't empty now . . .

I spotted Mum and Dad coming in. They were looking worried, as though they suspected I might be about to embarrass them by doing something silly. (How right they were!) But when they sat down next to Tabby, my dad's face lifted. (Tabby had that affect on people.) And in a moment or two he had Mum chuckling as well.

Then suddenly it was time. Ruby hauled me to my feet and we stood there, two small skinny children in front of a room full of grown-ups. I wiped my sweaty palms on my trousers and swallowed hard. I seemed to have lost my tongue. You would have too . . . I mean, how were we going to tell them? How were we going to make them believe us? And if they didn't, then in just two days time, these people would get the shock of their lives!

CHAPTER 10

'Thanks so much for coming,' said Ruby, her cherry plaits bobbing wildly. 'Davie and I have got something very exciting to tell you.'

I nodded, but was still too shy to speak.

'You see, a couple of days ago we found an old newspaper . . .' Ruby nudged me and I held it up. 'It's called the *Darkington Times*.'

A few people craned their necks to see it. Annie Button and her sister-in-law (who looked just like Ruby – red hair and wild eyes) were in the front row. They read some of the headlines and their eyes popped out!

'Pass it round,' said Ruby, handing it to Mrs Hunter – a grey-bunned lady who owned the town's last surviving hotel. 'And you'll see it's a very strange paper full of ghost stories and creepy stuff. Me and

Davie thought it was a prank at first; a joke for people who like to dress up in Halloween costumes . . . but then we found out it's actually for real.'

Someone laughed at the back. Others tutted. But Ruby ignored them.

'You see,' she said. 'One article really caught our eye. It's a list of horrible places to go on holiday . . . and well, we thought we could put an advert for Middle Spit Sands in there. Not that it's horrible here, of course,' she added, spotting Old Joe's stern face in the crowd. 'But we thought we could pretend it's the sort of place that people who like ghosts and ghouls and witches and stuff might like to go to on holiday. So, anyway, me and Davie wrote an advert for our town and we were about to send it to this paper when it got lost. Only it didn't. Somehow it made it into the paper all by itself – it just sort of appeared there, as if by . . . well, magic, we think. You'll see it there on the back page.'

Mrs Hunter nodded. And then she stood up, and read our advert out loud. There were a few sniggers at the back. And a few more stern faces near the front, especially Ruby's mum, who was frowning darkly at her daughter. But Ruby ignored her.

'Anyway,' she carried on cheerfully. 'That was when the messages started coming.' Ruby nudged me, and I realised it was my turn.

'Er . . . that's right,' I mumbled. 'The messages were from people who wanted to book rooms. But they didn't come in the post, they just sort of appeared out of thin air.' I deliberately didn't look at anyone in the room, especially my parents, whose eyes were boring into me. 'The first one appeared written in sugar sprinkles that I dropped on the kitchen floor.' I swallowed nervously. 'Then there was one in my soup bowl. And another on the bathroom mirror . . .'

There was confusion now on some of the faces. Others just looked cross. I could see Dad shaking his head and Mum looking glum. A few people were rolling their eyes.

And then I understood – not one of them believed us. Of course they didn't. I wouldn't have either – would you? They thought we were making it all up, telling silly stories. Then a few people started to whisper: 'Total rubbish!' and 'Over-active imaginations!' and Ruby's face turned red.

'It's true!' she yelled. 'Honestly it is!'

Old Joe stood up. 'Well, if it's true, where's your proof? Where are these messages then? Let's see them.'

'You can't,' I said miserably, realising how silly we must sound. 'They disappear as soon as I've read them.'

'What rot!' said Old Joe. 'You're wasting our time.' He shook his head and muttered, 'Bloomin' kids!' Then he picked up his hat to leave.

Mr Blair the grocer stood up too. 'It's a great story. Perfect for Halloween, when it comes . . . and you've done a cracking job making the newspaper and everything. But we've had enough now.'

'Please believe us!' I squeaked. 'It's true. These creatures really are coming. In two days time, at the next full moon, dozens of them will arrive in Middle Spit Sands, thinking they have a booking . . .'

More laughter. More tutting. More cross faces. And then the scraping of chairs as people got up to leave.

'Wait!' I shouted. 'Stop! We need to get the town prepared.'

'Enough, Davie.' It was my dad. He and Mum were on their feet too. 'You've had your fun. But no one's coming here. They never do . . .'

But just as he spoke, the back door of the hall

suddenly burst open and a wild gust of wind ripped through the room, sending the *Darkington Times* whooshing off someone's knee and up into the air. Then a woman stepped through the door, put down her suitcase and caught the paper as it fluttered gently into her arms.

'You know, you really should listen to them,' she said in a rather posh voice. 'Because if you don't, you won't be ready in time. And personally I wouldn't like a lot of unhappy creatures stomping through my town on a full moon!'

I gaped.

Ruby gawped.

And the whole room froze.

Then the woman grinned at us. 'Hello, everyone. My name's Agatha Gum.'

She clicked her fingers and the door snapped shut behind her. Then she stalked through the hall, ignoring the sea of bewildered faces around her. I was one of them. I couldn't take my eyes off her. It wasn't that she looked odd, exactly. She was a small neat lady – about my mum's age – with shoulder-length blonde hair, pink apple cheeks and pale blue eyes that glittered mischievously when she blinked. But it was the glow that shocked me – a purple sparkly aurora that hung around her shoulders like a shawl, scattering glittery bits of static that hissed when they hit the floor.

'Davie Hart, I presume,' she said, taking my hand with a firm grip. 'What a pickle you and your friend have got yourselves into,' she giggled. 'Never mind, we'll soon sort it out. It's not every day I get to help create a ghost town . . .'

And a dozen jaws dropped open.

CHAPTER 11

Everyone was so shocked they sat down and shut up. And Agatha Gum took charge. She walked around the room looking us up and down. 'You're probably wondering who I am,' she said. 'Well, let me explain. I'm Agatha Gum, editor of the *Darkington Times*. And I can't tell you how excited I am to be here.' She gave us all another huge smile. Then continued walking around. 'I was thrilled to receive your advert – delivered,' she added lightly, 'by Mist Wisp Mail.' She turned to me. 'The blood on the envelope made it travel so much faster, Davie – you're such a clever child!'

I blushed, and she winked at me.

'The advert was most intriguing,' she went on, 'because ghost towns don't exist any more – not real ones where we can relax and be ourselves . . .' She looked sad for a moment. 'A long time ago there were many such towns – I holidayed in them, as a girl. But most have been bulldozed to make way for modern houses for modern humans.' She glared at us for a moment, and then her face softened. 'So I booked a room here, to see your town for myself. But I couldn't wait for the full moon, so I decided to come early. And it's just as well I did because there's so much to do, and so little time to do it.' Everyone looked at her and nodded – as though this was a perfectly sensible conversation to be having in the lifeboat hall on a wet Wednesday morning.

'But making a ghost town won't be easy,' said Agatha earnestly. 'It's true; your town is deliciously dark and dingy. And the weather is wonderfully awful too. But the details aren't quite right. Everything needs roughing up a smidge. You need more dust . . . spiders, rats and bats. And tidy attics will need a jolly good messing up. And then there's the shops,' she said with a smile aimed at Mr Blair. 'Special people need special things. And the same goes for the café,' she twinkled at me.

Everyone in the room was transfixed (or bewitched, perhaps), including my parents. Everyone, that is, except one person . . . and that person was now struggling to his feet with a face like thunder. 'Now wait one minute, young woman!' he growled. Old Joe had been listening with increasing anger, shuffling his feet and chewing his lips. He wasn't someone that liked change. And he couldn't contain himself any longer. His face was white. His eyes slits of black. 'You can't just come marching into our town and tell us what to do. We like it here just the way it is. We don't want you – whatever you are – or your strange friends. Ghosts don't exist. And if you're nuts enough to think they do, you need a doctor's help not a holiday!'

But just then there was a sudden CRASH! at the back of the room. A window shattered, scattering glass across the floor. And an arrow whistled past my nose, landing with a THWHIP! in a window frame next to me. Everyone gasped. Even Old Joe looked shocked. And for a second no one moved. But I knew exactly what this was . . .

'Careful, Davie,' called Mum. 'Mind the glass.'

Gingerly, I stepped through the broken pieces and reached out for the arrow. Just as I'd expected, there was a rolled-up piece of paper wrapped around its shaft. 'It's another message,' I said nervously. Carefully, I pulled the paper off and unrolled it, and before it could disappear I held it up for everyone to see – thick, creamy parchment with loopy black handwriting and a waxy seal at the bottom of the page. Then I read the message:

LORD HAROLD DE BONVILLE,
OF WOODSTOCK PARK,
POLITELY REQUESTS
CHAMBERS COMMENCING
THE FIRST GOOD MOON
OF THE MONTH

I felt a shiver scuttle along my shoulders. It was him! Headless Harry himself. The dead knight from the story in the *Darkington Times*. Then the words vanished, leaving a blank piece of paper that crumbled in my hand.

Agatha's eyes twinkled. 'He's such a rogue.'

'That arrow could have killed someone,' said Mum

crossly. 'And look at the mess he's made!' (That's Mum for you – who cares about spooky messages from the dark underworld, when there's a mess to be cleaned up?)

'Oh, don't worry, my dear,' said Agatha. 'He'll pay for the damage, I'm sure. Indeed all your new friends will repay you well for your hospitality . . . in gold.'

'Gold?' It was the grey-bunned lady – Mrs Hunter – who'd spoken. She stood up now and turned to face Old Joe. 'I think we should listen to this lady, Joe. What does it matter where these people come from, or what they think they are? As long as they've got good manners and they don't make a mess of my dining room . . .' (She looked pointedly at the broken window.) 'then they're welcome in my hotel. It's a matter of life or death for this town now; without customers we're finished.'

Joe shook his head crossly. 'But there are no customers, don't you see? It's all a big joke – a set-up to make you look stupid!'

Agatha rolled her eyes and sighed. Then a familiar voice from the back of the room spoke up.

'But what if it's not a joke?' It was Tabby Toot. He was standing now too, towering over everyone else.

'This lady could be offering us a future, Joe; a way for Michael and Sheila to keep the café going. And for George to keep his grocer's shop open and Helen to keep her hotel. It could even mean something for you too, Joe – maybe you could get a new donkey . . .'

The words fell likes stones on the floor. No one had ever dared suggest Joe should replace Doris. It was the final straw.

'I want no part in this!' he snapped. 'You can all do as you choose, but I won't be involved.' And with a final glare around the room and a scowl at Agatha, he stomped out of the hall, banging the door loudly behind him.

For a millisecond no one moved. Then Tabby walked down to the front. He reached out one long (quite hairy) hand. 'Welcome to Screaming Sands, Miss Gum. Tell us exactly what we need to do to save this town, and we'll do it.'

And so it began.

CHAPTER 12

'Before we do anything I need to know two things,' said Agatha, rummaging in her handbag for a rather sparkly pair of blue spectacles. 'How many rooms are available, and how many bookings have you received so far?'

The first question was easy. Of the once many hotels and guest houses in town, only Mrs Hunter's hotel and Annie Button's bed & breakfast were left. And between them they had just twenty-four rooms (twenty at the hotel and four at the B&B).

Agatha raised her eyebrows at the small number. Then turned to me. 'And bookings?'

Ruby grinned smugly as I pulled out the notebook. 'About sixty five, I think. But that doesn't include the message on the arrow.'

Agatha peered over her spectacles. 'Good gracious,' she said. 'And who knows how many more might just turn up without booking.' She sighed. 'Where on earth are we going to put them all?'

'There's a campsite on my farm,' said Tabby. 'Room for at least a dozen tents, maybe more.'

I was shocked. I didn't know he had a campsite. It was impossible to believe any tent could withstand the howling gales up at Tabby's place.

'And I've got Glenda's keys,' said Mrs Hunter. 'She owns the guest house next to my hotel. She's in Australia visiting her sister but I'm sure she won't mind if we use it.'

'We can use this hall too,' said Mr Blair.

'And what about the caves?' I said. 'One of the messages specifically asked for a cave.'

'Oh yes!' breathed Ruby, her eyes wide with excitement. 'There's loads round the point. I can show them to you, though some get cut off at high tide . . .' Ruby's mum shot her daughter a look, one which I suspected said: 'How come you know so much about those dangerous caves, when I've told you not go anywhere near them!'

Agatha grinned. 'The caves sound perfect! You'll be able to charge lots for them.'

Everyone exchanged glances. But it was Dad who was the only one brave enough to ask. 'Er . . . excuse me, Miss Gum, but who exactly are these people we've got coming?'

I looked closely at my dad and felt my heart lift; there was a sparkle in his eyes. And his face was suddenly alive with hope. I felt a wave of joy sweep over me too.

'Well, Mr Hart,' said Agatha, glancing at my list of bookings, 'to be honest you've got quite a mishmash . . . most of the names I know, as they subscribe to the *Darkington Times*. But there's a couple I don't recognise. Once word gets round, it's hard to stop, and news of a real ghost town would be too exciting to keep secret.'

Agatha looked down at the list again. 'First of all there's Darkly Sage. He's a lovely chap, a vampire – he drives the blood bus – you know, the bus that goes round taking blood donations for the hospitals.'

I felt an elbow in my ribs from Ruby. Her eyes were like dinner plates. 'A vampire!' she breathed.

'Then there's Jack Snow . . .' Agatha went on. 'Such a talented chap – plays piano, sings, dances, tells jokes too – though his is rather a tragic tale, I'm afraid to say. You see a long time ago, when he was still alive, he was a famous entertainer. But somehow he got himself stuck inside a theatre cupboard right at the end of the summer season and no one found him until the following year, by which time, of course, he'd literally starved to death.' Agatha sighed. 'So he's all bones now.'

I gulped. So he was the chatty skeleton in my mirror.

Agatha went back to the list. 'You've also got the O'Hara sisters.' She made a face. 'Not known for their humour that lot. They're banshees,' she added. 'They foretell death. They wail their heads off whenever someone's about to die!'

I shuddered, and hoped I'd never hear *that* sound! Then Agatha gave a sudden little squeal of excitement. 'Emerald Green! What fun!'

Everyone looked blankly at her.

'Mistress Green,' she said, pointing at the list. 'She probably sent her cat with the booking. She's quite a powerful sorceress, you know, a bit of a show-off sometimes, but a real good egg, an animal lover. And, I don't like to gossip, but she's always had a bit of a soft spot for Harry.'

'Harry?' said Mr Blair. 'Who's he?'

Agatha rolled her eyes. 'Harold de Bonville, the chap who sent the arrow message. He was once the most famous knight in England – a jousting champ – until the day he got his block knocked off. A terrible thing to lose your head, and I must say he's rather hot-tempered as a result. But old Harry enjoys a party – he's great fun! You'll love him, I'm sure.'

I glanced at Dad, and was relieved to see the sparkle was still there. He was grinning too. In fact everyone was, which was rather odd. Here we all were, sitting in our little town hall, learning about a load of crazy spooks who were heading our way, and no one looked the least bit bothered.

Agatha meanwhile was thumbing through the rest of my list. 'Poltergeist. Orb. Ghoul. Gray Lady . . .' She glanced up. 'That's Lady Jane May. A lovely old stick, though terribly forgetful. She has a cat – pees everywhere; very stinky. Now then . . . two goblins, three trolls, two hags, a kitchen witch . . .'

'What's a kitchen witch?' asked Ruby. 'Is that different to an ordinary witch?'

Agatha tutted. 'There's no such thing as an ordinary witch – most witches specialise.'

Me and Ruby looked at each other blankly. So did the grown-ups. Agatha rolled her eyes. 'If you had foot fungus would you go and see an eye doctor?'

'Er . . . well,' stuttered Ruby.

'Well it's the same with witches. Most of us specialise. Of course, there are a few general spell botherers but their magic is usually quite thin, like jam spread over far too many sandwiches.'

'What sort of witch are you?' asked Tabby with a chuckle.

'Can't you tell?' she sparkled at him, her aura flashing brightly for a moment. 'I'm a list witch of course.'

Tabby shrugged and Agatha raised her eyebrows. 'A list witch is an organiser. I'm terribly organised, don't you think? I remember everything and everyone I've ever met. I use spells to make things happen. I can read people's thoughts too. And move things around with my mind.' To demonstrate she glanced at a window and it shot open, letting in a gust of icy cold wind. Then she blinked and it slammed shut again.

'Wow!' breathed Ruby.

Some of the grown-ups looked scared now, as they realised once and for all that this was no joke.

'What other types of witches are there?' asked Ruby.

'Oh, far too many to mention.'

'Tell us a few . . . please.'

Agatha sighed. 'Well there are sea witches, mist witches, bad-weather witches, switch witches – they are quite fun; they can switch things around, you know, turn a dog into a cat, or a frog into a mouse . . . that sort of thing.'

Ruby's face glowed. 'I wish I could do that.'

I was relieved she couldn't, or I'd probably be scurrying around under the floorboards somewhere with a tail and whiskers!

'There are witches for everything, even sewing – they are stitch witches, of course. There are also rich witches who specialise in alchemy and snitch witches – terrible sneaks who are always spying on others. Then there are the sorceresses, like Emerald Green, the lady who sent you a message via her cat . . .'

'What do sorceresses do?' asked Mrs Hunter nervously.

'Necromancy, mostly.'

'Pardon?'

'Oh, you know, bring things back to life . . . zombie makers.'

The room suddenly froze. Opening windows and organising things was one thing, but bringing things back from the dead was . . . well, just a bit scary (super scary, in fact). I could see Ruby was desperate to know more, but then Mum coughed . . .

'Who else is on the list?' she asked, changing the subject from witches.

Agatha gave her a quick smile. 'Yes, well, let's see . . . witches, werewolves . . . oh and Sad Susan.'

'Sad Susan?' said Mum. 'Who's she?'

'It's a dreadful story . . .' Agatha began. 'Susan is a weeping wraith; a ghostly bride. She got killed on her wedding day. One minute she was bouncing up the church path all set to wed her beloved, the next she was dead, stone dead – the church steeple had fallen on her head.'

'That's awful,' I gasped.

'Yes, especially as her fiancée decided to marry her younger sister that same afternoon.'

Everyone was appalled.

Agatha shrugged. 'Susan's a lovely girl but still rather desperate to find a husband.' She winked at Tabby. 'So watch out if you're a single chap or she might take a shine to you and stay! Now, where was I . . . ?'

Agatha continued rattling through the list, telling us who, or rather what, was coming, until she reached the end. 'So all in all, a perfectly lovely group of guests,' she beamed.

'Are you sure?' asked Mrs Hunter with a worried face. 'I mean we've all enjoyed hearing about these . . . er . . . people. But are you sure they aren't, well . . . dangerous?'

Mr Blair nodded. 'I've seen the movies – vampires biting your neck, ghosts giving you a heart attack. Not to mention wild werewolves rampaging around the town.'

'Mr Blair, my dear man,' said Agatha – her eyes shining with mischief. 'When you go on holiday, do you pop into other people's shops and spend your time rearranging their shelves and selling their carrots? Or you, Mrs Hunter – when you go away, do you rush around other people's hotels making beds and arranging dinner? No, of course you don't. And neither will these creatures. They will be on holiday; they won't be doing their usual stuff. They will do the things holidaymakers do. There's certainly nothing to be alarmed about. And anyway, what makes you so sure you don't have creatures like these living here already?'

'What?' Mr Blair frowned. 'In Middle Spit Sands? Well, I think I'd know.'

'Would you? Would you really? How can you be sure? Granted, some look a bit different.' She grinned. 'You'd probably pick out a skeleton if he popped in to buy a pound of spuds. But vampires? Werewolves? And witches? They don't look any different to you, or me, Mr Blair.' Agatha's eyes sparkled with mischief. Then she gave a small giggle and turned to me. 'Now, young Davie, I think we'd better put another advert in my paper, don't you, to let our readers know that Screaming Sands is fully booked until further notice!'

CHAPTER 13

And it was. Every bed in town was taken. Even spaces that didn't have beds . . .

'Cupboards or drawers will do for the orbs.' declared Agatha. 'And attics and cellars will suit the spooks.'

It was the following day and she was touring the town, making sure we were turning Middle Spit Sands into a real ghost town. Everyone was mucking in (apart from Old Joe who was still sulking in his caravan). Instead of cleaning up and cleaning out we were making a mess. And Agatha had given us strict instructions on how to do it. Dirt and dust were to be encouraged. All cleaning products were banned. Air fresheners too. ('They bring us out in a hideous rash,' warned Agatha.) Lamps were to be replaced by candles. ('The undead adore candlelight,' breathed

Agatha. 'So flattering for pale skins!') Draughts were to be made bigger. Windows forced to rattle. And all taps made to leak! ('Spectres love the drip drip of a leaky tap,' said Agatha dreamily.) Dad and Tabby had been out with their toolboxes since dawn, making sure all Agatha's suggestions were followed. And now it was Mrs Hunter's turn to have her hotel inspected. Me and Ruby had gone along to help . . .

'More mould!' said Agatha, wrinkling her nose at Mrs Hunter's clean little dining room. 'I can't smell a trace of it. And make it damper in here. Throw a few buckets of sea water on the walls and open the windows to let the rain in.'

Mrs Hunter grimaced. She'd spent her life trying to keep the damp out of her seaside hotel and now she was being told to encourage it! But she didn't argue. No one argued with Agatha.

'Let's look outside,' said the witch, swishing out of the dining room and into the hall. 'Not nearly enough dust,' she declared as she passed the reception desk. 'You can't welcome the undead without dust on your desk!' Then she marched through the front door and immediately her face fell. 'Good Lord, where's the ivy?'

We all looked up. There wasn't any. Mrs Hunter's hotel was naked apart from its nice white pebbledash front. 'I've only just had it painted,' she moaned.

'Well, it won't do – not at all. The undead will expect a bit of ivy climbing the walls. It's lucky I'm here!' Agatha rummaged in her pocket and produced a small green packet. 'Poison ivy powder – fast growing. Sprinkle it on the window ledges. But only a smidge or you'll have a forest by lunch time!' Then she turned to us. 'Right, next stop Mr Blair's shop.' And we were off again.

'Er . . . Agatha,' I said, jogging to keep up with her. 'How did you know we'd need stuff like that powder?'

'A list witch is always prepared. I never travel anywhere without a few home comforts.'

An hour later, after inspecting the grocer's shop (not enough candlelight), Annie Button's guest house (too clean) and the post office (too tidy), it was the café's turn to be checked. As soon as she stepped inside Agatha's nose wrinkled in disgust. 'Where are the cobwebs?'

Mum, who was on her hands and knees making sure the corners were nice and dusty, gave a sigh. 'I've been searching for spiders to make cobwebs all morning.'

'No matter,' said Agatha, rummaging in her pocket again. She produced a small black box which she handed to me.

'What is it?'

'Freeze-dried spider eggs . . . just add a few to a pan of boiling water and they'll start popping out like corn.'

'Wow!' breathed Ruby. 'That's so cool!'

'Yes, they are cool,' said Agatha cheerfully. 'They're needle spiders – absolutely super spinners. They'll have this place webbed-up in minutes!'

I gulped. I didn't want to tell Agatha I was scared of spiders.

'But you only need a few,' she said firmly. 'They're big blighters once they've popped. And it's very easy to make too many . . . perhaps I should show you.'

But she didn't get a chance because just then Tabby stuck his head through the door. 'Er . . . Agatha, I think you'd better come quick . . . Mrs Hunter's in a bit of a pickle. She's rather overdone the poison ivy. She can't open her front door.'

Agatha rolled her eyes and followed him out.

'I'll help you with the spiders,' said Mum, reaching for the box. But as she did, the phone started ringing. 'Just give me a minute,' and she headed upstairs to answer it.

But Ruby was too impatient. 'Come on, Davie!' She snatched the box from my hand and dashed through to the kitchen. By the time I got there she was already reaching for a pan.

'Don't you think we'd better wait?' I said. I was no expert, but needle spiders sounded serious.

'Don't be such a wimp. Agatha said it was like making popcorn and I've done that loads of times.' In minutes she had a pan of water heating on the stove. As it began to bubble she opened the box. 'They don't look very exciting.'

I peered in. She was right. They were small and black, a bit like carrot seed.

'Oh well,' said Ruby. 'Worth a go, I suppose.'

I gasped as she poured half the box into the pan. 'Hey! Agatha said we only needed one or two.'

But it was too late. Ruby had the lid on the pan and the heat turned up high.

'What harm can it do?' she said, bobbing her cherry plaits in excitement. 'We can always send a few over to Mrs Hunter's hotel!'

But just then there was an almighty BANG! from inside the pan, like a firework going off. Me and Ruby hit the floor, just as another one went off which blew the pan lid sky high. It landed with a clang next to us. And then there was another BANG! And another. Loads more in fact. BANG! BANG! BANG! BANG! It was like a cowboy shoot-out. I shut my eyes and covered my ears. BANG! BANG! BANG! BANG! BANG! BANG! BANG! over and over again. It seemed to go on for ever (though it was probably only a few minutes). And then suddenly the gap between the bangs began to get bigger until finally they stopped. I hardly dared look. But as I opened my eyes something scuttled past me. I gasped. It was a spider, but not like any spider I'd ever seen before. It was enormous – about the size of my fist, and strangely see-through, like it was made of glass. As it scuttled past, its legs made an eerie tinkle-tap noise on the tiles. I shuddered. But as I stood up I saw something even worse . . . 'Ruby!' I gasped. 'Look!' The cooker was a wriggling, writhing mass of spiders. There were hundreds of them. And more still spilling out of the pan, scuttling off along the work surface, climbing the fridge, jumping into the sink, tinkle-tapping their way all over the kitchen.

'What have we done?' I gasped

Ruby's face was a mixture of horror and fascination. And for once she was speechless. In fact we both just stood there, surrounded by the crazy critters, tinkle-tapping around us.

And then . . . 'Oh pants!' I whispered. 'They've started spinning.'

They had. In what felt like seconds, the stove was covered in a sparkly white web.

'Oooh,' said Ruby. 'That's pretty.'

It was. Like expensive net curtains. Except I wasn't sure my parents would like their cooker covered in net curtains. But there was no time to worry because just then I felt a tingle at my feet. I looked down . . .

'Ruby!' I gasped. 'I'm being webbed!'

A gang of spiders were spinning threads around my ankles. I watched in horror as they circled around me, like they were playing some crazy spider game of Ring a Ring o' Roses. I tried to move but my ankles were now welded together. I reached down and tried to flick them away, but as soon as I got one off, another three joined in.

'Run, Davie!' shouted Ruby.

'I can't run!' I said through gritted teeth. 'My legs are stuck together!' And then more spiders appeared and soon my knees were webbed together too.

'I'll save you!' yelled Ruby. But as she lunged towards me, she realised she was being webbed as well.

'Help!' she squealed.

I wanted to say, 'Good! Maybe that'll teach

you to ignore a witch's instructions!' But I was too busy fighting off spiders myself. Dozens of them were scuttling up my body now, fighting for space; each one spinning faster and faster. In minutes they had webbed my arms to my sides.

'Help!' I yelled. 'MUM!'

I looked around desperately for something to stop them. But the kitchen was completely webbed. And me and Ruby – with only our heads uncovered – were beginning to look like Egyptian mummies!

'MUM!' I yelled again, louder this time. 'WE NEED YOU! NOW!'

But it wasn't Mum who came stomping into the kitchen. It was Agatha. She rolled her eyes and shook her head. 'Kids!' she muttered, as though we were a couple of messy toddlers who'd just had a food fight. Then she said a few weird-sounding words under her breath and the spiders who were now spinning around my neck suddenly stopped. Frozen like statues. I felt a cold sensation spread across my body and realised the webbing had turned to ice. I shivered. And it cracked, falling to the floor in a large, icy sheet. Agatha flicked the frozen spiders off me, crunching a couple under her heel. Then she did the same to Ruby. 'Seems like Mrs Hunter wasn't the only one who went a bit far,' she muttered as she flicked the last spider off Ruby's head.

'Sorry.' Ruby scuffed her feet. 'It was my fault.'

Agatha shrugged. Then smiled. 'Do you know, I rather like the kitchen like this? What do you think, Davie?'

I looked around. Everything was ice. It was how I imagined an igloo would look. Huge icicles hung from the ceiling. The table and chairs were frozen solid. And the floor was like a skating rink.

'It looks like we've been hit by an Ice Age,' I said. 'Freaky. But cool too!'

'I agree,' beamed Agatha. 'All we need now are a few sabre-toothed tigers or perhaps a mammoth or two.'

I wasn't sure if she was joking.

CHAPTER 14

'Thankfully she was joking. And the kitchen began to thaw out after a few hours. And while it did, me and Ruby spent our time spreading needle spiders around town (carefully controlled by Agatha this time) and delivering dirt bombs, which were my favourite. They looked like little grey deflated balloons, but when you blew them up they floated away, then suddenly burst open, scattering dust and dirt and bad smells around the room.

Tabby had a good idea too. He'd bought a pile of pumpkins off a pal who had a farm a few miles up the coast and he suggested we make pumpkin lanterns.

Agatha was slightly sniffy. 'That's just silly human Halloween stuff,' she said, but seeing as Tabby had gone to the bother of fetching them, she agreed to prepare them for us. It was amazing to watch. She carved them with her finger – up, down, backwards, forwards it whizzed around, and in seconds a face would begin to form. And then in another few flashes it would be finished. Each one uniquely ghastly, like little orange gargoyles.

We put them all over town – on walls, in windows, on cliff ledges and even on the sea rocks. Agatha said she'd 'light' them later.

When she'd finished with the pumpkins, Agatha sat down with Mr Blair to tell him the things he'd need to stock in his shop. She gave him a long list of items with super spooky names like deadly nightshade night cream, snakeroot shampoo, blister-bush bath foam, turtle-spit toothpaste . . .

The café menu had to change too. 'You'll need to offer plenty of raw meat for the vampires and wolves,' said Agatha. 'Hop-grog for the goblins, and herby salads and soups for the witches.' She gave Dad strict instructions about how to make them. But it was Mum who volunteered to gather the poisonous plants and disgusting bugs we'd need.

The town was buzzing with an excitement that I'd never felt before. It was as if everyone could finally see a way to put Middle Spit Sands back on the map. And they were going all out to do it. Even the most unlikely people got involved – Mr and Mrs Broom, a quiet retired couple who lived on the edge of town, said they'd not only rent out their spare room to one of the new visitors, but they'd offer art lessons too.

'Oh they'll love that,' breathed Agatha. 'Especially the vampires, they're so creative . . . I can just imagine it – night painting on the cliff edge, with a howling wind around your head. Lovely!'

Mr Broom looked a bit alarmed by the plan, but he agreed to give it a go. Then Mrs Hunter's brother, Jock, a round, smiley sort of a man who ran the bar in her hotel suggested he offer boat trips in the bay.

'A midnight sail across the spiky rocks? How toe-curlingly exciting!' said Agatha. 'Count me in!'

The only person who still wasn't happy was Old Joe. He skulked around the town sucking his teeth and shaking his head, watching and growling, as Middle Spit Sands morphed into the much shabbier, far dirtier, cobweb-covered Screaming Sands . . .

It was nearly midnight on the night of the full moon. Everyone in town was crammed into the café (apart from Old Joe). Me and Ruby had been dozing in the corner when Agatha gave us a gentle shake and said it was time.

'Why do they all want to arrive on a full moon, anyway?' yawned Ruby, as she helped set up a table outside the café where we'd greet the guests. As usual the weather was wet and wild and a salty wind was blasting into my face.

'Because, dear, that's when our energy levels are at their highest,' breathed Agatha, whose aura certainly seemed brighter than ever – the glittery bits stung my skin when she brushed past me, but I didn't mind too much because at least it provided a bit of light. Agatha had confiscated my torch. 'It's not very welcoming to have a beam of light flashed in your face,' she had said. Agatha had also confiscated every camera in town. 'Taking a photo of a ghost will kill it,' she said glumly. 'And it gives the rest of us a hellishly awful headache!'

Ruby and I put some final touches to the café, then at last we were ready.

Me and Agatha sat at the table outside, waiting to welcome our ghastly visitors. I blew on my hands to warm them up. I must admit, I was the most nervous I'd ever been. My teeth were chattering. My stomach was spinning. And my face was set in a ghastly grimace. But there was no sign of a moon, full or otherwise, let alone our guests. The only lights I could see were from the winking pumpkins that glowed like strange orange dots around town.

I was just about to raise this problem with Agatha when suddenly it happened. WHAM! Just like that! A spotlight was turned on in the sky. The clouds parted and the full moon beamed down on us, covering the town in a bright white glow. The jagged rocks in the bay sparkled menacingly. The cliffs glowed green and the pumpkin lanterns cast strange new shadows that flickered spookily in the wind.

'Wow!' I breathed, looking around in wonder. The light made the town look sort of beautiful (in a freaky-beaky, mad, bad, dangerous-to-know sort of a way). Agatha smiled and her aura glowed even brighter, then I felt her hand on my arm. 'Here they come, Davie,' she whispered. 'Isn't it exciting!'

And it was.

At first I saw nothing. But as I stared into the darkness, black shapes began to form. I thought they were bats at first . . . and then I realised I was right! It was a huge flock of them flying in close formation, heading straight for us. But just before they reached us, they parted and darted away, and behind them larger shapes began to appear, people-sized shapes! Some were sitting on things – carpets, sticks . . . a bicycle! Others were simply walking through the air as though it were a field. I noticed lights appearing on the cliff tops too. And a few vehicles began driving slowly down the hill into town. I tried to breathe – but somehow I couldn't. And then the first of the sky walkers landed with a small thud on the main street in front of us. It was a tall figure, swathed in a black cloak. The face was hooded so I couldn't tell if it were a man or a woman. But as it got closer it hesitated briefly, as if checking it was in the right place. I glanced up too and saw our new sign hanging above the café window (courtesy of Agatha). The Poisoned Kettle café, it said, written in old-fashioned loopy writing. Reassured, the figure strode over.

'Good evening, Yarrow,' said Agatha warmly. 'It's a fine night for flight.'

The figure nodded, and then swiped back its hood . . . and I jumped. I couldn't help myself, because there was no head there. Nothing! Not a jot! Then suddenly a face began to appear, just like the picture on my nan's old telly, which takes a few minutes to warm up. At first the face was barely formed, but I could vaguely make out a nose, a chin and two sharp eyes – eyes that were boring into me.

'Don't worry, Yarrow,' soothed Agatha. 'The boy is a friend. They're all friends here.'

And as she spoke, Yarrow's face grew stronger, until it was fully formed and sort of normal looking (in a transparent sort of way). Hair appeared too, a thick thatch, dark red in colour. It was quite a nice head really (all things considered).

'Greetings,' the figure said, nodding at me.

'Hello,' I squeaked.

Agatha, meanwhile, was scribbling in a book. I read the name she'd written – Yarrow and next to it she'd added – sky-walking spectre. 'We've booked you a tent, Yarrow – up on the cliff. Terrific gales. Very cold. Great view of the stars. You'll love it.'

Yarrow bowed, and then rummaged in his pocket for a moment before pulling out a small black bag, which he tossed towards us. It landed with a thud, spilling gold coins on to the table. For a second I wondered if they were real. But Agatha was more matter of fact. She carefully counted out three of the coins, then closed the bag and handed it back to the spook. 'Thank you, Yarrow. That'll do nicely. Now, Davie, go and fetch Tabby and tell him that his first guest has arrived.'

As I opened the café door, a blast of light and warmth poured out, and the shy spook immediately began to fade away. But when Tabby stepped outside, smiling broadly and offering his hand, the sky walker rallied and his face returned.

'Follow me, sir,' said Tabby cheerfully. 'Do you have any bags?' There was an awkward moment as the spook looked at Tabby and he looked at me, and everyone sort of shrugged. I mean, what would a ghost keep in a suitcase? But Tabby just smiled and said, 'Follow me,' and then he and Yarrow disappeared into the night. I didn't envy him. Friendly or not, I wouldn't want to go walking up to his big field with a dead person behind me! But there was no time to worry because just then I heard footsteps and voices, and I realised a queue of sorts was starting to form. I looked along it, taking in all the crazy-looking creatures that were beginning to line up, and suddenly I felt like laughing. It was as though a Halloween party had just ended and everyone was trying to get on the same bus home.

CHAPTER 15

'Move along there!'

'Stop shoving!'

'I was here first!'

In fact, there was quite a lot of argy bargy going on; pushing and shoving and arguing.

'Witches hate queues,' whispered Agatha. 'But banshees are the worst.'

And they were. Three tall women in flappy black dresses were pushing their way through the line. They had sharp elbows and big feet. And they each pulled a metal suitcase on wheels, which they used to bash people out of the way, run over toes and force their way to the front of the queue.

'We were here first!' snapped one; the tallest woman with the longest nose.

'Yes indeed,' snapped the second. She was shorter but more stocky.

'And we won't wait a moment longer!' growled the third. The smallest, but by far the crossest looking of the three.

'We are the O'Hara sisters,' they said together. 'And we don't like queues!' And as if to emphasise the point, they all stamped a foot simultaneously, then stood glaring down at us. I felt as small as a snail but Agatha wasn't the slightest bit afraid.

'Welcome, ladies, everything's ready. If you'll just settle your bill in advance.'

'What? Pay before we stay?' snapped the first.

'Outrageous!' said the second.

'Impossible,' added the third.

But Agatha was adamant. (She'd already warned us about banshees. Tight as a clam shell, she'd said. Always looking for a way not to pay. If you don't get the money when they arrive, you'll never see a penny.) She folded her arms and refused to budge on the matter. The sisters folded their sharp, bony arms and refused to budge either, while the rest of the queue began to grow restless; shuffling their feet and whispering.

Eventually, Agatha outstared them.

'All right – have it your own way,' snapped the first sister.

'But we'd better have a good time!' added the second.

'Or there'll be trouble,' growled the third, producing a small purse from her pocket. As she opened it, several tiny bats fluttered out, squeaking and spitting. The banshee slowly emptied a few gold coins on to the table. Equally slowly, Agatha counted them, while I kept my head down and tried not to meet anyone's eyes. And then finally: 'Okay, Davie, you can fetch Mrs Hunter,' said Agatha, 'she'll show the sisters to their hotel.'

Which, to be honest, was a total relief! For a moment I thought they might be staying at our café – and there's no way I'd have been able to sleep, knowing that lot were next door!

I didn't envy Mrs Hunter as she marched the sisters away. But as she told me later, she'd had years of experience dealing with awkward customers. And she wasn't the least bit bothered, even when they accidentally (on purpose) bashed her heels with their suitcases, as she led them briskly through town.

It was much quieter without them. And I actually started to enjoy myself. The next guests were two young giggly witches in high heels and smart frocks (a switch witch and a kitchen witch, according to Agatha). One of them took a bit of a shine to me and blew me a kiss as she tottered off with her friend to find Mrs Hunter's hotel.

An odd-looking orb came next. The size of a tennis ball, it just sort of hovered around like a bad smell. It had no face, or none that I could see, so it couldn't speak. But the two small wraiths who appeared to have travelled with it, chatted away as though it understood every word. Perhaps it did. It bounced off happily enough, heading for a broom cupboard at Tabby's place, which it would share with the wraiths.

And then Darkly Sage made his appearance. I'd been dreading this moment. He was the vampire whose message had appeared in my soup. I'm not big on vampires. All that biting and blood drinking. I was expecting a tall man in a black cloak with big teeth, but Darkly Sage was small, younger than Dad, with kind brown eyes and a rucksack on his back. And he actually looked quite normal (in a bright white sort of a way). I wouldn't really have minded if he'd had our spare room, but he'd booked a cave, so Mrs Hunter's brother, Jock, led him off to get settled in. (He and Tabby had kitted out a dozen or so caves with cosy sleeping bags, flasks of tea and complimentary packs of ginger nut biscuits! Vampires love ginger nuts, apparently.

Meanwhile, me and Agatha carried on with the queue. Werewolves, witches, goblins and trolls – I met every monster you've ever lost sleep over. But the mermaids were probably the weirdest of all. Merrows, as Agatha called them. Halfway through the night, they showed up in the bay, splashing and flashing their long whaley tails, before rolling up on to the shingle. As they left the water, their tails turned to legs and they staggered up the beach like toddlers learning to walk. There were four of them. But it was impossible to tell if they were boys or girls. They all had long hair that they hid behind shyly as they stood swaying and blinking in the light (smelling pretty badly of fish). A little later Jock rowed them out to the sea caves, where he'd laid out welcoming trays of sushi.

At some point, Mum came out with some tea for

Agatha and a mug of hot chocolate for me, but we were so busy I don't remember drinking it. And then suddenly everything stopped. I think I actually fell asleep at the desk because one moment I was watching a cheeky orb who was bothering a witch by buzzing around her head while she searched for her purse, when suddenly I felt a hard clunk on my head as it hit the table! I had finally collapsed with exhaustion. Then, in what seemed a blink of an eye, I was tucked up in bed and dreaming happily – not of ghosts or ghouls or anything else the slightest bit scary – but of super-sized ice-cream sundaes with cherries and swirls and hot fudge whirls . . . it was blissful. But as usual it didn't last long!

CHAPTER 16

'Wake up, bog head! You're missing all the fun!'

After what seemed like just five minutes of blissful rest, I opened my eyes to find Ruby's grinning head, looming over my bed.

'Come on,' she said, poking me hard, in the chest. 'Get up!'

I groaned and pulled the duvet over my face. 'Go away! I'm too tired.'

But Ruby wasn't having any of it. She grabbed the edge of my bedclothes and with a big, hefty tug, yanked them (and me) right off the bed and on to the floor.

'Hey!' I yelped, trying to give her a whack as I went. But she dodged out of the way.

'You won't believe what's happened!' she said.

'The town is packed. Absolutely jammed tight. It's amazing! Come and look.'

She danced over to the window and drew back the curtains. Reluctantly, I hauled myself up and followed her over, squinting at the daylight that now poured into my room. I looked out . . . and gasped. And then gasped again. There were people . . . everywhere! (Okay, okay, I know that the sight of people isn't strange or unusual, but it is in Middle Spit Sands.)

'And that's not even half of them,' squealed Ruby, jumping up and down with excitement. 'Agatha says most of them won't come out again until dark.'

I couldn't stop staring. It was so weird seeing our town full of visitors. They were everywhere, and doing all the normal things that you'd expect at the seaside. Some were playing games, sitting in deck chairs, eating ice creams, snoozing or just gazing out to sea. Others were clambering over the rocks with buckets and spades – rock pooling maybe? And right out in the bay I could just about see Jock's boat bobbing about in the waves, packed with people. It was odd. Middle Spit Sands looked just like any other seaside town. Apart from the fact that everyone was dressed in black or purple. And they were enjoying themselves in the pouring rain!

I giggled. We'd done it. We'd actually gone and done it. Me and Ruby had finally found our town some customers. I had to stop myself from throwing my arms round her. (I blame lack of sleep.)

'Anyway,' she said, heading for the door. 'Your dad says you've got to get your lazy bones out of bed and get yourself down to the café immediately. It's getting busy down there and they need your help.'

I punched the air with joy, and then not even caring if Ruby saw me, I started getting dressed as quickly as I could. I had customers! Real customers!

I took the stairs three at a time, and very nearly crashed into Dad . . .

'Thank heavens!' he said, handing me a huge tray piled high with dirty dishes. His hair was standing on end, and there were dark circles around his eyes. But he was also grinning like mad. 'Get this lot into the kitchen quickly while I take another order.' Then he bustled off back into the café.

I found Ruby in the kitchen about to start washing pots. She rolled her eyes when she saw the tray. 'Hells teeth!' she muttered. Then she threw me a tea towel. And for the next few hours we worked like ants. There wasn't even time to talk. But eventually Dad tapped me on the shoulder and handed me the order pad.

'Ice creams, son!' he winked at me.

And finally I got my first look at the customers.

Mum, who was standing at the counter, making up bills, smiled as I came into the café. 'Table nine,' she said, nodding at the window table.

I looked about in wonder. I'd never seen the place full before. Every table was groaning with customers squashed in, elbow to elbow. Some were standing, leaning against the walls sipping their drinks; others were waiting outside, queued up along the front. Thankfully, most of them looked quite normal, in a black-clothed, white-faced kind of a way. It was mostly witches and hags along with a few trolls, slurping their tea from saucers and some big hairy blokes who were chatting in the corner (I guessed they were wolves). The Merrows were there too, sitting near the door. Just as well really, because in the heat of the room, I'm sorry to say, they smelt bad, really bad, like a very dirty fish tank!

I squeezed over to table nine where Darkly Sage, the cave-loving vampire was sipping a cappuccino and reading a book on pot holing. I tried to ignore the plate of raw steak that was sitting in front of him, but as I came closer, he stopped reading for a moment and speared a piece with his fork. As he tucked in, a tiny dribble of blood trickled down his chin, which he caught with his long white tongue!

Next to him sat the two giggly young witches from the night before (thankfully they were only eating ices) and across from them was a tall thin bloke with his back to me. I couldn't tell what he was because he had a big floppy hat pulled down at the back. But as I reached the table he suddenly turned to look at me and I very nearly fell over. He was a skeleton! Honestly, he was. Just sitting there, quite the thing, a big bunch of bones grinning horribly up at me.

'Ice cream, ice cream, we all SCREAM for ice cream!' shouted the skeleton.

'Er, okay,' I stammered.

He slapped me on the back delightedly. 'Jack Snow is the name! And you must be Davie Hart. Sorry I missed you last night, young feller. I was late, see! Got bogged down in a bit of fog.' He stuck out a long bony hand towards me, and I shook it nervously. (I was terrified it would come off in my hand!)

'Do you like jokes, Davie . . . ?'

'Er, well . . .' I was actually finding it quite hard to speak. But Jack didn't seem to notice.

'Okay then, here's a good-un . . . Why didn't the skeleton go to the party?'

'Pardon?'

'*Because he had no body to go with!* No body to go with! Get it?'

The two witches gave a titter. And Darkly Sage looked up from his steak and smiled.

'Okay, here's another – keep up now! What musical instrument does a skeleton like best?'

'Er . . .'

'*The trom-bone*, of course! Boom Boom!' And with that, he pulled off one of his legs and pretended to play it like a trombone, while the foot part dangled horribly at one end. My mouth dropped open. My eyes boggled his bony leg, and I felt a slight lurch in my belly. The witches, meanwhile, were in stitches. Darkly gave a deep chuckle. And even Agatha, who was clearing a nearby table, was grinning. And then suddenly I giggled too. I just couldn't help myself. There was something very likeable about Jack Snow. And actually, when you got over the whole bony thing, he wasn't the least bit scary. Not really.

'Okay, Okay,' he said, now balancing his leg bone

on his hat. 'How do skeletons keep in touch with their pals?'

I shrugged.

'*By tele-bone!*' he yelled, flipping his leg bone up in the air, catching it again and then holding it up to his ear like a phone. 'Hello, hello, is that Napoleon Bone-apart?' he grinned. 'What would you like for lunch, my old ship mate – spare ribs maybe?' He ran a (bony) finger along his own ribs, playing a tune, as if his rib cage was a xylophone.

The two young witches were roaring with laughter now and Darkly Sage was chortling too. In fact, lots of the customers were.

Jack stood up and took a bow, to much applause, then he collapsed back into his seat and glanced again at the menu. 'Okay, young feller, I suppose I'd better order something. Now then, let's see . . . I'll have a Doris please . . . whatever that is.'

So I told him all about Doris. About how she'd walked the beach for years, how she was the oldest beach donkey in Britain, and how unfortunately she'd dropped dead just over a month ago. Jack seemed genuinely sad about that.

'That's a real shame,' he said glumly. 'Sounds like she was quite a character.'

I noticed a lady, who was sitting at the next table sipping salted-nettle soup (Dad's special of the day), was listening too. She was dressed entirely in green. 'Excuse me,' she said, catching my eye. 'But is that the donkey on the postcards in the shop?'

I nodded, noticing a familiar black shape sitting on the chair next to her. A cat – a black cat – the talking black cat I'd met two days ago!

'So sad,' said the lady, dabbing a jade-coloured hanky to her green eyes as emerald-coloured tears sparkled down her cheek . . . and then instantly I got it. This was Emerald Green, the sorceress who loved animals. She swept her curly red hair off her face. 'Perhaps I could have a Doris too,' she said. 'In her honour.'

In the end several tables ordered one, including everyone on Jack's table. And back in the kitchen, as I unpacked the banana puffs, I realised how weird events had turned out to be. Here I was making ice-cream sundaes named after a dead donkey for a bunch of scary monsters. And the strangest bit of all was that it didn't feel strange. It actually felt quite brilliant!

After that I didn't get much chance to talk to the customers. I was too busy taking orders. I was too busy taking orders. My ice-cream sundaes were really popular. And I even had to ask Ruby to help me. It was as if the customers thought our food was somehow a bit unusual – foreign maybe – and because they were on holiday they wanted to try as much of it as possible. So I spent the next two hours making dozens of Dorises, Fizz Bangs, Volcanoes, Sea Swamps, Haunted Houses, Choc Logs and Bat Splats (a new recipe I'd invented featuring liquorice and cherries). Dad, meanwhile, was run off his feet cooking the savoury food – all the usual dishes, and new stuff too! Masses of raw meat concoctions for the vampires, as well as witches' brews and stews . . .

But at last the queues got shorter and the tables began to empty, and the lunch-time rush was over. Finally, Dad told me and Ruby to take a break. And we were free to go outside and see what was happening in our town.

CHAPTER 17

There were so many people on the pavement we had to dodge past them as we headed for the beach.

'Still no sign of Headless Harry,' said Ruby, taking a good look around. 'Agatha says he's probably lost his head again.'

As we stepped on to the shingle, a small ball landed at our feet. Ruby picked it up and threw it back to a bunch of big hairy guys who were playing rounders nearby. As we watched, a beardy bloke who was trying to reach base before the other team balled him out, suddenly turned into a wolf, right there in front of us! One minute he was a man (big and hairy, but definitely a man) the next he was a wolf (all legs, teeth and shaggy coat). He pounded down the beach and beat the ball by miles!

'What a cheat!' said Ruby crossly. As she spoke, 'the wolf' snapped back into a man-shape again to celebrate his victory. Weird!

We carried on walking. In another corner of the beach, two trolls were playing chess on a board they'd drawn on the sand. Instead of chess pieces they were using old bones and seagull skulls . . . I thought it was a bit yucky myself, but Ruby loved it.

Further along, I could see a couple of witches flying a kite – a small black kite with red stripes. Except it wasn't a kite. When I looked closer I realised it was a . . .

'Dragobat!' said Agatha appearing by my side. 'Lovely, isn't it!' she giggled.

It *was* pretty amazing. About the size of a large bat, it had the head of a dragon, with bat-shaped wings and little flames that popped out of its mouth as it swooped and flapped around the sky. I couldn't take my eyes off it.

But there was other odd stuff to see too. Beach Frisbee, where no one actually used their hands. The witches playing were using magic instead. There was also a goblin sandcastle-building competition. (Just so you know, goblins aren't green at all. They actually look a bit like trolls, who look a bit like us, except they're smaller. Goblins are even smaller than trolls. And much, much sneakier. If a goblin ever asks you to play Twister, don't! Not only do they cheat, they pinch too. But their sandcastles were amazing – enormous towers with interconnecting tunnels and intricate turrets, moats and even a drawbridge or two . . . But they didn't last long – the goblins kept knocking each other's walls down and tunnelling under so the floors collapsed.

Every so often a fight would break out, and suddenly there would be a great big wriggly ball of angry goblins wrestling and whacking each other.

Agatha rolled her eyes and looked about to intervene when suddenly she sniffed the air. Her eyes narrowed and she turned sharply towards the cliffs. I turned too, and in the distance I saw a tiny plume of purple smoke billowing softly into the sky. A dark shadow passed over Agatha's face and her aura bristled crossly. 'If that's what I think it is . . .' She turned and stalked off across the sand.

'Wait,' I called. 'What is it?'

'Necromancy!' I heard her mutter.

Me and Ruby glanced at each other. 'What's she on about?'

Agatha didn't stop, but she yelled back angrily: 'Someone's raising the dead!'

Me and Ruby looked at each other again. Raising the dead? But there were no graveyards in Middle Spit Sands . . . and then suddenly it hit me. 'Doris!' I whispered. Hers was the only grave in town. And that was where the smoke was coming from – her grave, in the field at the bottom of Tabby's place.

Ruby made a face. 'They wouldn't . . . would they?'

We took off after Agatha. But by the time we'd caught up with her, she'd already reached the bottom gate into Tabby's big field. The smoke was thicker now. And darker. It smelt of violets (a bit like toilet cleaner). I covered my nose with my arm, and closed my eyes as we fought our way through the fug.

And then suddenly we saw her. It was Emerald Green, the sorceress from the café. She was sitting in a deck chair around a fire, right next to Doris's grave. She smiled and waved and gave me a cheery thumbs up!

But Agatha wasn't amused. 'Now look here!' she snapped, hands on her hips, her aura blazing. 'This is private property . . . you can't just come along and start digging up dead donkeys.'

But it was too late. As she spoke, the ground around us began to shake and shudder, like a mini earthquake. The sky turned black, there was a deep roll of thunder, followed by a scissor-sharp crack of lightning and a few drops of rain. I shivered. It was almost like a re-run of Doris's funeral!

Emerald Green was on her feet now, doing some sort of crazy dance. Her head bobbed backwards and forwards and her arms made weird shapes. She started to chant too – total mumbo jumbo that I couldn't make out.

The thunder and lightning grew louder. And the rain got heavier. And my teeth began to chatter.

Ruby hid behind her hands. Only Agatha didn't move, her stony face fixed on Emerald. Then I noticed Doris's grave start to shudder, and suddenly the ground split open. I held my breath, not wanting to look, but somehow not able to close my eyes either. And then I heard it. The sound of those darn bridle bells again.

Only louder now, like they used to sound when Doris was walking along the beach.

Emerald's dance got wilder and the hole in the ground got wider and wider and wider until I couldn't bear to look any more . . . and then suddenly everything stopped; the chanting, the dancing, the thunder and

lightning. I opened my eyes a smidge and watched as Emerald reached down into the grave. And then I saw it – a head – a big old familiar donkey head, which emerged out of the hole,closely followed by the rest of its body. Doris had come back from the dead!

CHAPTER 18

As zombie donkeys go, I reckon Doris didn't look too bad. True, there were a few maggots clinging to her ears. Her tongue was sticking out a bit and her legs looked wobbly. But all things considered she looked pretty tip-top. Except for her eyes. They were a strange burned-orange colour, unfocused and swirly. One minute they'd fix you with a glare, a bit like the old Doris used to do, then suddenly they'd dart away – up, down, round and round like windmills. It was actually quite scary. I was just wondering if I should point out this problem to Emerald when suddenly there was a yell.

'HOY!'

I turned and my heart plopped into my wellie boots. A familiar figure was shuffling quickly across the field.

'Hells teeth,' gasped Ruby. 'It's Joe!'

I wasn't sure whether to make a run for it. Ultimately this was my fault. But Joe didn't seem to spot me. As he drew level he just stumbled past, his face fixed on Doris, tears steaming down his cheeks.

'Doris? DORIS! Doris, my old sweetheart,' he rasped. 'What have they done to you?'

I was just about to apologise. Apologise for everything. The advert. The newspaper. The dozens of crazy creatures swarming around town. Not to mention the bringing back from the dead of his beloved donkey, who now stood swaying in front of him, crazy eyes and all. When suddenly Joe threw his arms around Doris's neck and started sobbing. But they weren't tears of sadness. They were tears of joy!

Me and Ruby watched in wonder as Joe stopped hugging Doris and shook Emerald Green wildly by the hand. Then he kissed her. The witch looked quite shocked and I wondered if Old Joe had remembered to put his teeth in. Then he kissed Doris again. Then he went over to Agatha and kissed her too. Me and Ruby were next. Thankfully he didn't kiss us – just patted our heads and ruffled our hair and called us 'rascals'. Then he shuffled back to Doris and showered her with more kisses and cuddles.

At that point I felt a hand on my arm. It was Agatha, and she was beckoning me and Ruby to leave Joe and Doris to it, which I was quite glad about because I felt a bit odd; sort of sad and happy all at the same time. And I certainly didn't want Ruby to see me cry.

As we walked back down the hill I thought about everything that had happened in the last few days. And I realised that finally everyone in Middle Spit Sands was sorted. Mum and Dad had got more than enough customers to keep the café busy. Mrs Hunter's hotel was full. Mr Blair's shop was going great guns. And even Old Joe had got his Doris back (in a wonky-donkey kind of a way). And that's where my story might have ended. Happily Every After-ish. Except it didn't, of course, because something was about to happen that none of us knew about. A bad creature was heading for Middle Spit Sands that was far more frightening than any of the ones that had already arrived. It wasn't a wolf or a witch or ghost. It was something much worse . . . it was an estate agent!

You see the café was still officially for sale. And right at that moment the man who Mum had asked to sell it was on his way to Middle Spit Sands.

Roger Pilkington-Smith, prided himself on being able to sell anything to anyone. He was the richest estate agent in Sunny Bay (the big town further along the coast), and there was no house or business he couldn't flog to someone. Indeed, it was him who'd sold the Whistling Kettle café to us in the first place, and it would be him who would sell it on to another set of 'mugs', sorry, buyers (all for a tidy sum for himself, of course). Buyers like Ned and Sherry Bruce, a kindly old couple who wanted to set up a tea shop in their retirement, and who were currently sitting in the back of Roger's shiny new Range Rover.

Roger couldn't have been happier. He was a born and bread Sunnysider (that's what people who live in Sunny Bay call themselves). And like all Sunnysiders, he rather enjoyed the fact that Middle Spit Sands was going down the toilet. Unlike Sunny Bay, which was big and busy and had loads to offer – two theatres, a cinema, a bingo hall, and loads of fancy restaurants and bars. Not to mention a brand-new pier (which Roger Pilkington-Smith owned). The sun always seemed to shine in Sunny Bay too. A fact Roger Pilkington-Smith was probably rather glad of, as he drove swiftly down the rainy road into Middle Spit Sands.

Meanwhile in the Whistling Kettle café, there was chaos. Me, Ruby and Agatha had raced back to break the news about Doris, only to find the café heaving with customers. And right in the middle sat the O'Hara sisters, tapping their feet and complaining loudly about how long they'd had to wait for their order.

'It's outrageous!' shouted the tallest banshee, waggling a gnarled old finger at me, as if it was my fault. She was dressed in a shiny black velour tracksuit with matching trainers (obviously her holiday clothes).

'Unbelievable,' agreed her sister, who was similarly dressed with her hair in bunches.

'Unforgiveable!' snapped the third sister, who was also wearing a tracksuit, along with a strange straw hat with a rat's skull stuck to the top. They tossed their heads and glowered at everyone around them.

'Thank heavens,' said Mum, as we appeared. 'Davie, go and help your dad with the sundaes. Ruby, can you help me clear these tables?'

I wanted to tell Mum about Doris right away, but I didn't get the chance. We were suddenly swept up in the hustle and bustle of jobs and customers.

I found Dad in the kitchen with his head stuck in the freezer searching for ice cream.

'They want Raging Volcanoes!' he yelled desperately. 'But I can't find the fizzing lemonade ice cream.'

I reached past him and took out a tub, which was tucked underneath a pot of Strawberry Snowbombs. I took the scoop from his hand and set about making the sundaes myself. I scooped out the ice cream, and finished them off with real lemonade and a cherry on top. Then I trotted off to deliver them.

'Thank goodness,' breathed Mum. 'They were getting so cross.'

In fact the sisters were hopping mad. Their faces were red. Their arms were folded. And I'm sure I could see real steam coming out of their noses. As I laid down the sundaes they shot me such a glare I could feel goose pimples popping up all along my arms.

'This had better be good,' said the first sister.

'Better than good,' added the second.

'The best!' snapped the third. 'Otherwise we might have to start wailing, and you know what that means!'

I smiled nervously, then backed away to take an order from a group of goblins who were having a sugar cube fight in the corner. Mum, meanwhile, was having a tough time at the cash desk with a hag who was haggling over her bill. Ruby was clearing up the mess left by two trolls. And Agatha was busy interviewing three hairy-faced wolf people about how they were enjoying their stay. (She had decided to write an article about our town's transformation for the *Darkington Times*).

And that's when Roger Pilkington-Smith made his entrance.

CHAPTER 19

The estate agent must have known something was wrong as soon as he'd arrived in town. For a start there were no parking spaces . . . anywhere!

Middle Spit Sands only has one tiny car park, and it's always empty. But not today. Today it was packed full of smart shiny sports cars (belonging to the rich witches). As a result Roger was forced to park his car in a ditch, much further up the hill, close to Old Joe's caravan.

As he and the Bruces walked down the road, they must also have noticed the hoards of dark-clothed people. And the black cats! (Roger hated cats, we later found out, because they made him sneeze.) And then there were the pumpkins, dotted hither and thither in the most unusual places.

Jock, Mrs Hunter's brother, who'd been out litter picking, had seen Roger and the Bruces arrive. He'd followed them down the hill and told us later how he'd heard Mrs Bruce remark 'how lovely' the pumpkins looked 'especially as it wasn't even Halloween yet!'

And then finally they'd arrived outside the café. According to Jock, Roger had looked at our new sign – the Poisoned Kettle café – and 'harrumphed' loudly. Then, shaking his head, he'd started to go inside when two yellow-toothed vampires standing at the front of the queue had told him to wait his turn. He'd 'harrumphed' even more at that. And had to wait a good ten minutes before he and the Bruces had been able to come in.

Jock reckoned it was just long enough for the old couple to decide that this café probably wasn't for them.

I was clearing tables when they arrived. As Roger Pilkington-Smith looked around the room, I saw his eyes nearly pop out of his head. The place was heaving! He glanced suspiciously at the strange-looking customers, then his gaze rested on the menu, chalked up on the board above the counter:

TODAY'S SPECIALS
Salted Nettle Soup
Deadly Nightshade Noodles
Hop Grog Goulash
Blooded Borsch
Frogspawn Soufflé
Poison Ivy Ice SCREAM!

Roger frowned. He peered around at the customers again – loads of hairy-faced wolfmen chomping down big (bloody) burgers, black-toothed witches sucking soufflé off spoons, and the vampires he'd met earlier, who were now tucking in hungrily to big bowls of dark-red soup – then he scowled. Finally he caught sight of Mum, who had appeared from the kitchen carrying a large tray of coffees.

'Mrs Hart?' he boomed in a not very friendly voice.

Mum was so shocked she dropped the tray. 'Mr Pilkington-Smith,' she squeaked, clasping her hand to her mouth. 'I forgot you were coming today!'

'Indeed,' said Roger crossly. 'You must have been too busy to remember,' he added in a vinegary voice.

After that things got a bit sticky. While Agatha looked after the café, Mum and Dad whisked Roger and the Bruces upstairs, where they told them that unfortunately the café was no longer for sale. The Bruces were secretly relived, especially as Mrs Bruce was sure she'd seen a skeleton lying on the sand as she looked out the café window! But Roger Pilkington-Smith was fizzing. Not only was he going to miss out on a sale (and the tidy sum he would have earned), but to see Middle Spit Sands so full of customers at the end of the season made his blood boil!

'Where have all these people come from?' he snapped, as a black cat wandered into the room, closely followed by three more.

'Er . . . it's a fancy-dress convention,' said Mum, trying to shoo the cats out.

'They booked the whole town,' added Dad nervously. (He's rubbish at fibbing.) 'Lucky, wasn't it!'

Roger sneezed (three times), and then gave them a hard look. He sneezed again. And again. And then he got up to go. As he walked back through the café he peered around suspiciously at the customers, who glowered back at him, almost willing him to ask them what they were doing there. Me and Ruby, meanwhile, stood in the corner holding our breath. As he walked past, Mr Pilkington-Smith gave me a nasty scowl and I shivered. There was something vaguely threatening about him. The look he'd given me was almost as bad as the banshees!

I stood in the doorway watching him walk away. But just as he reached the end of the street, a terrible thing happened. Old Joe appeared. With Doris!

There they were, dawdling through town, Joe shaking hands and talking to anyone who'd stop long enough to listen, Doris pausing every so often to drop strange-looking zombie dung bombs that vanished almost as soon as they hit the floor.

As soon as he spotted them, Roger stopped dead in his tracks. Everyone in these parts knew Doris. After all, she was a legend. They also knew she was dead. Dead as a dead beach donkey could be. (Which was usually pretty dead.) And yet, of course, now she wasn't. I nudged Ruby. 'Joe's going to tell Mr Pilkington-Smith about Doris. We've got to stop him!'

We raced along the pavement, but it was too late.

Roger was already by Joe's side, eying Doris suspiciously. 'Got yourself a new donkey, I see, Joe. What's her name?'

'It's not a new donkey,' grinned Joe. 'It's Doris! She's back from the dead.'

My heart sank. Ruby bit her lip and the Bruces looked at each other uncomfortably. But Joe wasn't finished . . .

'A lovely witchy lady dug her up for me an hour ago,' he grinned. 'Isn't it marvellous.'

Just then Doris's eyes started doing that spinning thing and a couple of big green maggots popped out of her nose. Mrs Bruce screamed. Her husband's mouth fell open. And even Roger took a step backwards. I don't blame them. No one likes maggots, do they? Especially not maggots that have just popped out of someone else's nose.

'That's disgusting!' said Roger looking like he might barf.

Joe scowled at him. 'Are you calling Doris disgusting?'

'Yes!' snapped Roger. 'And that beast can't be Doris. She's dead.'

'She was dead, but she isn't any more,' growled Joe.

Roger peered at Doris again (just as a third maggot made an appearance).

There was no getting away from the fact – this *was* Doris, and Roger recognised her straight away. He looked again, and frowned . . .

'But it can't be,' he said incredulously.

'Are you calling me a liar?' snapped Joe.

Sensing a scene, a crowd began to form. Witches and wolf people, a few vampires and, in amongst their legs, several goblins, skulking like naughty children looking for a fight, their tiny palms full of stones from the beach. Things looked like they were about to turn ugly. But just then the crowd parted and Agatha appeared, along with Tabby and Mr Blair.

'Hello, Roger,' Tabby said cheerfully, stepping between Joe and the estate agent. 'I haven't seen you for ages. Got time for a cuppa up at my place before you go?'

As he spoke, Agatha nudged me. 'Take Joe and Doris down to the beach, and stay there while we distract them,' she whispered.

We squeezed in between the grown-ups and gently guided Old Joe away from Roger and the Bruces. As we did, I heard Tabby say: 'Poor Joe, he's a bit confused today. It must be the worry about his new donkey – she's got worms, you know.'

But Roger didn't look at all convinced, and I could see him peering over Tabby's shoulder, trying to get another look.

Away from the crowd, Joe was smiling again. 'I don't know why he was so mean about Doris; she's lovely, isn't she?'

I was about to agree, when I felt a sudden sharp pain in my left shin. Doris had kicked me. And before I could complain, she turned and blew wind at me out of her rear end. Boy, was it foul. Zombie donkeys stink!

Holding my nose, I moved to the head end while we waited for Mr Pilkington-Smith and the Bruces to leave. I could see them lingering at the top of the beach, Mr Pilkington-Smith still staring suspiciously at Doris. Eventually, though, they headed off.

But there was trouble brewing, I could feel it. If Mr Pilkington-Smith found out what was really going on in Middle Spit Sands we'd be finished – he'd tell the world! I had a sudden vision of camera crews and ghost hunters descending on our town, trying to catch a glimpse of one of the creatures. Or, even worse, trap one. They'd want to put them on telly (which would kill the ghosts), or lock them in a laboratory and carry out horrible experiments on them. I shuddered. I couldn't let that happen. I liked the creatures (apart from the banshees). And besides, we needed them. Without the creatures our businesses couldn't survive. And then another thought popped into my brain . . .

'Ruby?'

'Mmmm?'

'Do you ever wonder where that copy of the *Darkington Times* came from?'

She frowned. 'What do you mean?'

'Well, it must have belonged to someone in Middle Spit Sands otherwise it wouldn't have been in our recycling bank.'

'Mmm'

'And if it belonged to someone here, then that must mean they're one of them.'

Ruby gasped. 'What? A ghost, you mean?'

'Or a vampire, or a witch or a wolf.'

As I spoke, I spotted Tabby tearing across the sand to join another rounders match – wolves only! And suddenly I saw Tabby like I'd never seen him before. Big, hairy, as strong as a horse . . . or a *wolf* maybe?

'It's Tabby,' I squeaked. And at that moment he suddenly looked up, as though he'd heard me. 'I think he's a wolfman,' I added in a quieter voice.

But before Ruby could reply I heard Mum calling. She was standing on the edge of the beach waving at us to come back. The afternoon was evaporating and evening was sweeping in, which meant a whole new crop of customers would be descending on the cafe.

'Hells teeth!' I said, glancing at my watch. 'The ghosts will be out soon!'

CHAPTER 20

In fact, they began to appear almost immediately; popping up like chicken-pox spots — orbs, wisps, wraiths and fully formed spectres. Ruby nudged me as a gang of trendy-looking teenage ghosts floated above us carrying picnic baskets.

Just in case you're wondering, most ghosts look a lot like us only flatter and greyer and a bit see-through. They also have a habit of fading in and out. So you can be standing on one, or sitting on one, without knowing it. Try not to. They hate to be squished — it makes them feel insignificant. They hate to be stared at too. But it was hard not to as we headed for home. In fact I was so busy staring at a group of acrobatic spectres who were doing some terrific tumbling gymnastics on the beach that I stood on Sad Susan!

'AAARGHH!' she squealed, as I realised I'd walked right into her, catching the hem of her wedding dress under my welly boot. She burst into tears. (Just in case you think you've missed something, I hadn't actually met Sad Susan before. She'd arrived long after I'd gone to bed. But I knew immediately it was her.)

'How could you,' she wailed, tossing her long black curly hair. 'Look at my frock, it's ruined!'

I looked. But it was pretty much ruined already, covered in blood stains down the front (from her accident with the church steeple, I presumed).

'I'm sorry,' I said. 'I didn't mean to stand on you.'

Ruby did her best to untangle the dress, but her hands just passed right through the fabric. Eventually Susan sorted it herself. Still sobbing she buried her head in her hands. 'I'll never get married now,' she wailed. 'You've ruined my day!'

'Don't worry,' I said nervously. 'You still look, er . . . lovely.'

Susan brightened. She stopped sobbing. And then smiled at me. 'Are you married?' she said batting her eyelids sweetly.

I gulped. 'Er . . . well . . .'

Ruby sniggered. 'Yes, he is,' she said beaming at Susan. 'To me!'

I was so appalled I couldn't speak.

'Would you like an ice cream?' I eventually squeaked, trying to change the subject. 'The café does fantastic sundaes.'

'Ooh, yes please. I love ice cream.'

Ruby and I looked at each other. We weren't sure a ghost could eat food. I mean, where would it go? It wasn't as if they had stomachs or anything. (It had been weird enough watching Jack Bones eat his ice cream. And for the record, in case you've never seen a skeleton scoffing ice cream before, he just sort of rubbed it on his rib bones. Very odd!)

The café was full again. But we managed to squeeze Sad Susan into a corner next to a stitch witch and a poltergeist. I couldn't see it, of course, because poltergeists are invisible. But I knew it was there because a teacup suddenly floated upwards off the table (to where its mouth must be), and then up-ended, pouring tea straight on to the floor. So *that's* how ghosts ate and drank! They didn't – it just ran straight through them!

Mum instantly appeared with a mop and bucket to clear up the tea, giving me a wink as she did. And Ruby handed Sad Susan a menu while I went off to find Dad. It was just as well I did because the kitchen was in chaos. I rolled up my sleeves to lend a hand just as Ruby returned with Susan's order: a Strawberry Fizz Bomb sundae. I set about preparing it as quickly as I could.

Afterwards, as I peeked into the dining room to see what she made of her sundae, it was pretty much as I expected – it all ended up straight on the floor. But she seemed to like the experience anyway, chatting cheerfully to others at the table about the wonderful wedding she was planning . . .

Meanwhile, the orders came thick and fast and by seven o'clock I was nearly asleep on my feet. So much had happened that day, which should have been whirring round my head. But to be honest, all worries about Roger Pilkington-Smith, or thoughts about who was the mystery owner of the copy of the *Darkington Times*, had long since gone, worn away by weariness. Dad was shattered too. He was leaning against the kitchen wall, his eyes shut, while Mum was suffering from an attack of the yawns.

They'd both been stunned to hear about Doris, but delighted too. 'I'm so glad Joe's got his girl back,' Mum had said with slightly watery eyes. The fact that Doris was a zombie donkey didn't seem to bother her. But they both shared my concerns about Mr Pilkington-Smith, though for Dad that was a worry for another day. He had more pressing matters to deal with . . .

'What are we going to do?' he said wearily. 'I know I wanted customers, but this is ridiculous.'

'And they'll be here all night,' added Mum, yawning again.

Just then we heard footsteps and Agatha appeared, followed by a shy-looking spectre in a white apron and cap. He twiddled his ghostly moustache and gave me a friendly smile.

'I hope you don't mind,' twinkled Agatha, her aura glistening. 'I took the liberty of placing an advert for some help in the *Darkington Times*.'

We gawped as the spectre. Was he the help?

'This is Alfonso,' said Agatha. 'He tells me he used to work here a long time ago.' The spook bowed. 'He will look after the kitchen this evening, so you can all get some rest.'

Dad looked a bit unsure. (I was too. Wouldn't you be?) But we were too tired to argue. And we headed upstairs gratefully (carefully avoiding two orbs and a small wraith that were playing tag on the bottom step).

As I went into my room I suddenly realised I'd forgotten to ask Mum who was staying with us. I was just about to go and find out when I heard a shuffling sound coming from my wardrobe. Then there was a thud, and a bang. And the door burst open and a small figure fell out. It was a little old lady in a long yellow frock.

'Goodness me!' she said landing in a heap. I reached out to help her up but my hand passed straight through . . .

'What on earth are you doing in here?' she asked.

'It's my room,' I said.

'Is it? Oh dear. Where is my room then? I seem to have mislaid it.'

'Er . . . maybe it's next door?' I said, pointing through the wall.

She brightened. Then nodded and walked straight through the wall. Just when I thought she'd gone, her head suddenly reappeared (which freaked me out a bit.) 'Thanks awfully!' she smiled. Then she vanished once more.

I blinked a few times, and shrugged. Then I climbed into bed (not bothering to wash or even undress – thankfully Mum was too pooped to check). I was just about to turn out the light when the Old Lady's head reappeared once more.

'Sorry to bother you again,' she said, 'but you haven't seen a cat anywhere have you?'

And then the penny dropped. This must be Lady Jane Grey. The Grey Lady Ghost who was always losing things . . .

I shook my head, and she sighed, then vanished back through the wall again.

At last I closed my eyes. And that's when I smelt it. Cat wee. Ghost cat wee? I sniffed. It was foul! And worse still, it was coming from right under my bed. But I was too tired to care. I stuffed my head under the pillow and was asleep in seconds.

CHAPTER 21

The next few days passed in a blur of busyness. My arms ached from scooping ice cream. My skin was wrinkled from too much washing up. And I was sick of the sight of chocolate sauce and sprinkles. But I was loving it too. Life was exciting! You never knew who, or what, might appear in the café next. Darkly Sage and Jack Bones were regulars now. And I'd have their orders ready before they set foot inside each day: rare steak sandwiches for Darkly – extra bloody, extra blue. And a double Doris sundae for Jack.

But always at the back of my mind, a shadow lurked. Roger Pilkington-Smith. I just couldn't shake off the feeling that something bad was going to happen. That somehow he'd find a way to burst our bubble of happiness. And then suddenly he did.

It happened one evening, a week after Doris came back from the dead. It had been another long day in the café and I'd nodded off on the sofa watching a film. When suddenly . . .

'WAKE UP! WAKE UP, DAVIE!'

I opened one eye and saw it was Ruby.

'Go away,' I groaned. I saw enough of her during the day.

'Davie, if you don't wake up right now, I'm going to fetch a banshee!'

That did the trick. I sat bolt upright.

'You've got to come quickly,' said Ruby, tugging at my top. 'Tabby's downstairs. A group of people from Sunny Bay are on their way over here.'

'What?'

'Tabby will explain . . . come on!'

As I got up to follow, she glanced at my feet. 'Do you always watch telly in your wellies?'

Downstairs, the kitchen was full of people – Mum, Dad, Tabby and Agatha. Ruby's mum and Annie Button were there too with Mr Blair and Mrs Hunter.

Alfonso meanwhile paid no attention to us at all. He just carried on cooking. I noticed he had a few helpers now – three ghostly waitresses in old-fashioned mop caps and aprons, who whisked off the grub to the waiting customers. Mad!

'It was a phantom hitchhiker who warned me,' Tabby was explaining. 'He's camping on my farm. He decided to head over to Sunny Bay today for a bit of a nose around and the driver who gave him a lift was on his way there for a meeting. Roger Pilkington-Smith arranged it. He's been spreading the news that Doris isn't dead.'

Everyone groaned.

Tabby nodded. 'Well, the hitcher went to the meeting too – he listened through the keyhole. Apparently no one believed Roger when he told them Doris was still alive, so he got angry and said they should come and see for themselves. So that's what they're doing. They're on their way here now.'

'At night?' said Mr Blair. 'Surely they'll wait until the morning.'

Tabby shook his head. 'That's the worst bit. Roger's been spying on us. He told the meeting he's been up here for the past few nights, watching our town from the cliffs above. He's seen everything – the spooks, the goblins, the skeletons, and Doris too, of course. And now the Sunny Bay people are coming to see it all for themselves, at night when we won't be expecting them.'

'How long have we got?' asked Dad.

Tabby shrugged. 'Half an hour, maybe less. There's a convoy of cars on the road according to the hitcher. And that's not all. Roger's called the local TV news station too.'

'Why?' gasped Mum.

'Because dead donkeys don't come back to life every day, Sheila.'

Mum rolled her eyes. 'But no one will believe him.'

'Maybe not,' said Agatha. 'But add the dead donkey story to what's happening here – a washed-up little seaside town that's suddenly full of unusual visitors – and you've got something worth filming.'

Instantly a horrible thought burst into my brain. 'But the television cameras will kill the ghosts.'

Agatha nodded.

'Then we've got to warn them.' I said, heading for

the door. 'They'll have to leave now – escape while they can!'

'I think it's too late for that,' called Agatha.

However, I wasn't listening. I was racing through the café. But as I stepped outside I stopped dead in my tracks. The town was heaving, even busier than before. Like Brighton beach on the hottest day of the year – except there were no pink-skinned lobster sun-worshippers. Our guests were lying about on the sand, lapping up the dark and the wind and the lashing rain. And there wasn't a centimetre of shingle to spare. Creatures were everywhere. Picnicking, playing games, sitting around campfires laughing and chatting together. I shook my head. Where would I start? How could I warn them?

I peered into the gloom, and through the shadows I could make out some familiar faces – the merrows, splashing around on the edge of the water, and Emerald Green and her cats (and rats!), sitting in a circle around a fire, singing merrily to themselves. There was other music too. A ghostly guitar band had set up near the top of the beach, hammering out a bunch of weird tunes with strange-looking instruments while other guests swayed spookily in front. I noticed the O'Hara sisters, Darkly Sage and Sad Susan among them.

'Word has spread,' sighed Agatha. 'Once ghosts hear there's somewhere safe to stay, they flood there . . .'

They certainly had. Every shape. Every size. From big floaty blobs to teeny weeny orbs. And in amongst all this weird chaos was Old Joe, walking proudly around the crowd with Doris, selling his postcards and chatting to the visitors.

'Agatha,' I said. 'What are we going to do?'

But she wasn't listening. She was peering up nervously at the cliffs. 'Look!' she said. And suddenly I could see them too – car headlights, snaking down, towards the town. The Sunnysiders were coming.

I looked around desperately for help. But Mum and Dad, who were standing outside the café now, looked as worried as me. Even Tabby, good old tough Tabby who never got stressed, looked terrified.

'Can't we just tell everyone to go?' I gasped.

'They wouldn't listen,' sighed Agatha. 'They're enjoying themselves too much. They trust all the humans here.'

Then I spotted my friends from the café, the young

switch witch and the kitchen witch. They were sitting on a bench, happily slurping ice creams. They gave me an idea . . .

'You said a switch witch can turn people into something else . . . well, why can't we use a bit of magic – get them to turn all the visitors into something else – pebbles or seaweed or starfish or something . . .

Agatha shook her head. 'There's too many.'

But I was already running over to the witch. In the distance I could hear the cars now. In less than a minute, Roger and his gang would see everything.

'Excuse me,' I said, tapping the witch on the shoulder. 'I'm sorry, but we need your help.'

She looked up, startled.

'We need you to turn everyone on the beach into something else.'

The witch gasped and her ice cream dribbled down her hand.

'Please,' I said. 'In exactly one minute a bunch of bad humans are going to show up with cameras. You need to hide everyone – NOW!'

She looked across the beach at the hundreds of creatures.

'All of them?' Her eyes widened. 'I can't!'

'Please,' I shouted. 'Please try.'

Her friend the kitchen witch patted her hand. 'I'll help, if I can.'

But the switch witch shook her head. 'There's too many.'

'Please,' I begged. 'You've got to at least try!'

She looked at the beach again, her face draining of colour. Then she grabbed her friend's hands. And they both shut their eyes tight, and the switch witch began to mutter some strange words . . .

But it was too late. Roger Pilkington Smith and the other Sunnysiders had already arrived.

CHAPTER 22

My heart sank. They'd caught us red-handed. But just then a sudden thick white mist dropped from the sky. And then there was a BANG! Like a rocket exploding. The candles and fires went out. And in an instant all the creatures changed.

'Hell's teeth!' gasped Ruby, who had appeared by my side. 'She's turned them into ice creams.'

I peered through the fog, and gasped. The beach was covered in sundaes! Banana Splits. Knicker-bocker Glories. Along with dozens of little cones stuck in the shingle.

'Oh dear,' said Agatha. 'I think the kitchen witch's magic has messed up the spell.'

I was so shocked I couldn't speak. I'd wanted her to change all the creatures into something realistic – stones or seaweed or starfish or something. But no, she'd turned everyone into an ice cream. I glanced at the switch witch. She was sitting very still. Her eyes closed, looking like she was holding her breath. The kitchen witch was in a similar state, still holding her friend's hands tightly.

'Don't disturb them,' whispered Agatha. 'If you break their concentration, the spell will stop.'

'How long can they stay like that?' I asked.

Agatha shrugged. 'Not long.'

'Hello Roger . . . what a pleasant surprise.'

Tabby was striding across the shingle towards the group, who were gawping at the ice creams in disbelief.

'What's on earth's going on here?' said Roger Pilkington-Smith. 'We heard music. And voices. Lots of voices, and then . . . this?' he gestured towards the beach.

'Oh, it's just us,' said Tabby in a jolly voice. 'Won't you come into the café for a drink or a bite to eat? It looks like it's about to rain again.'

A few of the Sunnysiders were nodding. But Roger wasn't budging. 'What's all that ice cream doing there?' he said. Which, given the circumstances, was a perfectly reasonable question. It was as though a mass picnic had suddenly been abandoned!

It was Dad who answered. 'The Whistling Kettle café is taking part in an ice-cream challenge,' he said not very convincingly. 'We're trying to come up with the largest number of sundaes ever made in one night. That's the judge over there.' He pointed to Agatha, who was walking across the sand to join them.

Roger rolled his eyes. 'That's ridiculous. I know what's really happening here. I've seen the monsters for myself!'

'Where's Old Joe?' asked a woman next to him. 'Roger was telling us some wild story about his donkey coming back from the dead.'

There were a few giggles amongst the group and Roger shot them an evil look. Tabby laughed too. 'Old Joe's got a new donkey, that's all,' he explained. 'He's called her Doris, in memory of the old Doris; perhaps that's why Roger's confused.'

'I'm not confused! Where *is* Joe?' Roger snapped. 'Then you can all see for yourselves!'

Tabby shrugged. 'I'm not sure. Perhaps if you come back in the morning.'

A few of the group nodded and looked like they were more than happy to go home. But just then there were footsteps and a blonde woman in a smart red coat appeared, along with a lanky man carrying a camera on his shoulder. 'Evening, Roger,' she said brightly. 'Hope we're not too late. Where's this dead donkey then?'

'That's Cathy Clarkson,' whispered Ruby. 'She's on the telly.'

I winced. So this was the news crew Roger had organised.

'There's no dead donkey here,' said Tabby with a chuckle. 'But we can offer you a lovely cup of tea in the café.' He turned, to lead the group away. But Cathy had noticed the beach full of ice cream. She nudged the cameraman . . .

Meanwhile, I glanced at the witches. They were still locked in their trance. But their hands were shaking now, and their teeth had started to chatter.

Cathy was peering into the mist. 'If there's no dead donkey, I might as well get a few pictures of the ice creams,' she was saying. 'If nothing else, it'll give us a bit of colour for the bulletins tomorrow.'

'No!' I gasped.

But it was too late. The lanky man had shouldered

his camera, and I could see him focussing on the beach. As soon as he turned it on, the ghosts would be gone, zapped into oblivion. And then I lost the plot. Really, I did.

I took off across the sand, waving my arms wildly and shouting as loudly as I could. 'NOOOOOO!' All eyes were on me, but I didn't care. Dodging ice creams and rocks and squidgy sea life, I powered over, ready to rugby tackle the cameraman, who was so shocked he just stood there, gawping at me.

But I never made it. Because right at that moment, there was an almighty clatter of hooves, and a huge black horse thundered down the street. A few of the Sunnysiders screamed. Even Roger looked shocked as the horse galloped down the pavement towards them. And sitting astride it was the strangest looking sight I'd ever seen. It was a knight! A real, live, super-shiny metal-man knight, head to toe in armour. He came to a clanking halt right in front of Roger and his gang, his horse rearing crossly in front of them, pounding its hooves and steam exploding from its nostrils. There were more screams and someone in the group appeared to faint slightly . . .

'Harry!' breathed Agatha. 'He's arrived at last!'

Headless Harry! My heart skipped a beat. It was him. The knight from the newspaper. Really it was. Except he wasn't headless – not yet, anyway . . .

As Agatha spoke, the knight pointed a metal arm towards the film crew. 'Put down that camera!' he boomed, his voice muffled somewhat by his visor.

The cameraman was as shocked as the rest of us. He just sort of stood there stupidly, too shocked to speak.

The knight was cross now. 'All right,' he yelled. 'You asked for it!' And then he did a terrifying thing. He flipped off his head (helmet and all!) and hurled the whole thing at the cameraman, Frisbee style!

Bonk!

It hit the bloke hard on the head, knocking the camera out of his arms.

'Good shot!' bellowed Agatha, which startled the witches, making them lose concentration and then . . .

BANG!

The mist lifted. The ice creams vanished. And suddenly the beach was awash with creatures again.

'Pants!' I muttered, as I was immediately surrounded by dozens of ghosts. I'm not sure who was the most shocked. The creatures. The Sunnysiders. Or the telly people . . .

Thankfully the mist dropped again, like a big heavy blanket, hiding the creatures from view once more. But it was too late. Everyone had seen them.

'Quick!' yelled Cathy Clarkson. 'Get down on that beach and get that camera running!'

Her lanky colleague did as he was told. But he'd forgotten about me. I was close now. And I threw myself at him, knocking the camera out of his arms again. Then I wrapped myself around it and clung on for dear life while the man desperately tried to wrestle me off. Then Ruby appeared and began kicking the cameraman's shins. 'Leave Davie alone!' she shouted. 'Go away! Leave us all alone!'

'Listen to the lady,' growled another voice. 'Be gone with you!' And I glanced up to see Headless Harry's head lying on the sand nearby, his eyes glaring crossly through the visor at the cameraman. Not that he noticed. He was still trying to pull me off his camera.

And then someone turned a hosepipe on us. At least that's what it felt like. Except it wasn't. It was rain. Sudden and explosive. It battered down, hard and cold like hailstones. Then there was an almighty rumble of thunder, followed by a pistol shot of lightning that was so loud I had to let go of the camera to shield my ears.

'Run for it!' yelled Cathy Clarkson. And the cameraman finally wrestled me off his camera, picked it up and ran across the beach, closely followed by Cathy and the Sunnysiders. As the rain lashed down even harder, the creatures vanished into the darkness too, leaving me and Ruby alone on the shingle. But we weren't alone. Because standing at the head of the beach was a strange-looking woman. She was tall and straight backed. Her hair was streaming out behind her, her eyes were closed and her arms reached up to the sky. She looked like she was conducting the storm. She was.

'Mum?' I whispered. It really was my mum.

I felt strong arms then as Dad pulled me to my feet and ran with me towards the café, while Tabby did the same with Ruby. As we ran, a fireball of lightning exploded in the sky, scattering hot coals on to the sand. And then the wind picked up and the sand began to spiral into patterns. I closed my eyes as it whipped faster and faster. Then as I peeped out again, I saw a massive black cone of wind hovering just above the bay – a tornado was building . . .

'Dad,' I yelled, as we reached the café. 'We can't leave Mum out there!'

He grinned at me. 'She'll be fine, Davie, trust me.'

And then finally we were sucked into the warmth and safety of the café.

CHAPTER 23

'I knew there was something fishy going on here!' snapped Roger Pilkington-Smith, as soon as the door closed behind us.

They were all there. The Middle Spitters. The Sunnysiders. The telly people and Agatha and the two young witches. Everyone except the witches were peering out the windows as the crazy weather raged outside. Cathy Clarkson was on the phone to her office, telling them about the twister that was currently spinning wildly out of control above us. 'We'll try and get pictures,' she was yelling over the noise. 'I've never seen anything like it. Save us the top slot in the late news bulletin!'

I peered out into the gloom, trying to spot Mum. What had she been doing on the beach? She looked super weird. What if she was swept away by the tornado? And Joe and Doris . . .

'Don't worry about your mum,' said a soft voice next to me. It was Agatha. She picked up my hand and squeezed it. 'And Joe and Doris will be fine too. I saw them heading for the caves with Darkly Sage. He'll look after them.'

As the wind whistled past the window, rattling the glass ferociously, I prayed she was right.

Cathy Clarkson meanwhile had cornered Tabby. 'So come on, tell me who all those people on the beach were, not to mention that crazy knight!'

Roger, who was sitting at the table next to them, leaned over with a nasty scowl. 'Yes, Tabby, who were all those unusual people on the beach tonight? Why don't you tell us what's *really* going on here?'

But it was Agatha who replied.

'They're weather watchers, if you must know,' she said. 'They follow storms. They knew there was a big one coming in, and they were waiting for it – quietly behind the big rocks,' she added, her eyes twinkling.

Roger made a face. 'Another load of piffle!'

But Cathy seemed strangely convinced. (Or

maybe Agatha was bewitching her. Or perhaps she just wanted a sensible answer to her question – after all, as all us kids know, adults never really believe in witches and vampires and creatures of the night, not really.)

'I've met people like that before,' said Cathy. 'They call themselves stormchasers. And they take their weather very seriously indeed.'

'Oh please,' growled Roger. 'Not you as well.' He shook his head. 'What about the ice creams? Where did they disappear to?'

But just then Cathy's cameraman gave a yell. 'Look at that!' he said, as another ball of fire burst in the sky.

'That's ball lightning,' said Tabby knowledgably. 'Very rare!'

'And very hard to do,' whispered Agatha, winking at me.

I frowned. What did she mean 'very hard to do'?

Roger scowled at Agatha and Tabby. 'You still haven't explained the knight.'

'I'm afraid that was Joe,' said Agatha with a sigh. 'He's not been himself lately – ever since Doris's death he's been acting very strangely. Dressing up, pretending to be other people. He thinks everyone's trying to pinch his new donkey too.'

It was totally unbelievable of course. Absolute poppycock. But it didn't matter. Because just then there was another shout from the window.

'It's snowing!' said Cathy. And it was. Thick flakes of real snow were drifting past the window now.

'Wow!' said Ruby, jumping up to look.

'Snow in August?' breathed Cathy. 'Now that's weird!'

'No, it's not,' I said. 'My birthday's the first of September, and there's always a few flakes around then.'

Then suddenly all eyes were on me. I blushed. They were looking at me like I was mad. Agatha gave me a knowing smile. And I felt a funny flutter in my belly. It was as though something was going on that I didn't quite understand. 'Where's Mum?' I asked nervously. 'I can't see her outside.'

CHAPTER 24

It snowed for another hour; just long enough to keep the humans stuck inside the café and allow the creatures plenty of time to pack up and go.

When the snow stopped, Cathy and her cameraman went off to get some pictures. 'If we hurry we'll make it back for the late night news,' she called as they headed for their car.

The Sunnysiders were ready to go too. They still weren't exactly sure what had happened, but the freaky weather was enough to send them running . . . dead donkeys didn't seem to matter any more.

Roger Pilkington-Smith was the only one who wouldn't leave. He stood outside the café, his arms folded, refusing to move another step. 'I know you're up to something,' he growled. 'I saw that donkey with my own eyes. And I saw those creatures on the beach. I'm going to expose you for what you are – a meeting place for monsters!'

'What monsters?' said Agatha. 'Monsters like those, over there?' She pointed to the shingle. And I gasped. Sure enough, a gang of strangers in black were standing on the sand peering up into the sky. For one terrible moment I thought Roger had caught us out . . . that some of our visitors hadn't escaped when they'd had the chance . . .

But no. These people weren't monsters. They were creatures of the night – but of the human variety . . .

'Hello there?' called one of them, giving us a friendly wave. 'We heard there's been a tornado here – we had to come and see for ourselves. This snow is amazing.'

Agatha smiled smugly at Roger. 'Stormchasers, Mr Smith. Would you like to come and say hello?'

But Roger had had enough. He stomped off muttering darkly to himself. As he went, I thought I spotted something following him up the pavement. The light wasn't good. I could barely see. But it looked rather like Susan. Sad Susan. Surely she hadn't taken a shine to Roger? Blimey! I wasn't sure who I felt most sorry for . . .

But there wasn't time to worry, because I'd spotted someone else among the rocks. Her hair was all over the place. Her clothes were wet. And her face was the colour of chalk. But she was still in one piece. 'Mum!' I yelled. 'You're safe!'

She came running towards me and threw her arms around me. 'Davie,' she breathed. 'Everything's okay.'

'But what happened?' I demanded. 'How did you survive the storm?'

Mum looked at me in silence for a moment and then her face softened. 'There's something I've been meaning to tell you, Davie,' she sighed. 'I'm afraid I'm a witch.'

And it was as if a thousand needle spiders had started spinning webs in my belly. My chest felt tight. I couldn't breathe. And that strange fluttery feeling flushed through me once more. 'A witch?' I gasped. 'But how?'

Mum squeezed my hand and then led me inside. And when everyone was settled and all the doors and windows were locked (in case Mr Pilkington-Smith returned), Mum spilled the beans.

'It's true,' she said solemnly. 'I'm a bad-weather witch.'

I was speechless.

'Wow!' breathed Ruby. Then she nudged me. 'Lucky dog! Imagine having a witch for a mum.'

'I don't practise,' said Mum quickly. 'But my mother was a witch. So I sort of inherited it. It's a bit like flat feet and sticky-out ears, I suppose.'

Agatha rolled her eyes. But Mrs Hunter looked

sympathetic and even Mr Blair patted her on the shoulder. (Meanwhile I was panicking. Had I inherited it too? I already had the flat feet and sticky-out ears.)

Mum sighed. 'I was never very interested in magic. And I stopped using it altogether when I was in my twenties.'

Dad nodded. 'That's true. By the time I met your mum she had left it all behind.'

'What about the snow on my birthday?'

Mum blushed. 'Well birthdays are special, Davie.'

'What else can you do?' asked Ruby, who was so excited she couldn't sit still.

Mum shrugged. 'Produce any form of bad weather – storms, mist, high winds, rain. Though I must say, Middle Spit Sands has never really needed my help before now. It has plenty of its own!'

I shook my head. It was all such a shock. But the more I thought about it, the more sense it made. No wonder Mum never liked having her photo taken!

'Will I be a witch?' I asked nervously. I wasn't quite sure I wanted to be. I mean, weren't witches meant to be girls?

Mum shrugged. 'Perhaps . . . I'm not sure. I didn't

get my powers until I was twelve. So we'll need to wait and see.'

'I can just see you in a pointy hat!' giggled Ruby.

I shot her a scowl and then turned back to Mum. 'Was it your copy of the *Darkington Times* that we found?'

She nodded. 'It must have got muddled up with the newspapers.'

'Which means that you must have known about Mum,' I said to Agatha.

'Of course, but it wasn't my secret to share.'

'Well I'm glad you're a witch,' said Ruby firmly. 'That tornado was fab! It really taught Roger Pilkington-Smith a lesson.'

Mum made a face. 'I'm afraid that wasn't all I did . . .' Her face turned red. 'Just before he went, I sneaked up to his car and poured some needle spider eggs into his engine.'

'What!' My eyes widened. Mum was never naughty.

Agatha giggled. 'With a bit of luck he'll be webbed up for weeks!'

Mum grinned. 'Or maybe Headless Harry will get him first. I saw him on the beach, looking for his head. Once he found it, he galloped off into the night, cursing the man who called in the TV cameras!'

Mrs Hunter, who was peering out into the darkness, gave a long sigh. 'But what do we do now? Everyone's gone. We're back where we started.'

It was true. All the guests had scarpered. Middle Spit Sands was a ghost town once again. But not one with ghosts in it. Just empty and bleak looking.

'They'll come back,' said Agatha. 'Once all this fuss dies down, I'm sure of it.'

But that could be months. The season was over. We all went to bed feeling dispirited. Especially me and Ruby. We hadn't saved Middle Spit Sands after all. We'd just caused chaos. And trouble. And all for nothing.

But not quite. I awoke the next morning to the sound of car horns. For a second I thought the whole storm thing hadn't happened, and the town was full of spooks again. I threw back the curtains and gasped. The town was full! But not with witches and wolves and creatures of the night. It was full of strange-looking people in anoraks. And as soon as I got down to breakfast

I discovered who they were. Scientists and weather watchers and bus loads of bearded stormchasers who stood on the shingle and marvelled at the snow and talked about the ball-lightning that had lit up the sky.

Of course, all the visitors needed somewhere to stay. So Mrs Hunter's hotel was full again. And so was Tabby's camp site. Even our spare room was occupied, by a young scientist from the met office who spent her days on the beach taking measurements and setting up experiments. Ruby was fascinated and followed the scientist wherever she went (getting in her way!). I was busy too, back making ice-cream sundaes in the Whistling Kettle café.

It was two weeks later. A Sunday. And Dad had decided to shut the café early. 'Give us all a well deserved rest,' he said.

Ruby was there. (She was like a bad smell – very hard to get rid of.) And so was Agatha. Unlike the other creatures, she had stayed on to finish the article she was writing about the town. But her case was packed and she was planning to leave soon.

I sat looking out of the window, feeling miserable. It wasn't as if the town was quiet. We still had a few weather watchers booked in. And not all the scientists had gone. But it just wasn't the same. I missed Jack Snow and his jokes. I missed Darkly Sage. I missed the giggly witches, and Emerald Green. Heck! I even missed the banshees (well, maybe not!).

'Cheer up,' said Mum, putting a tray of steaming hot chocolate down on the table. I tried to smile, honestly I did. But I couldn't quite do it. School was looming. One day soon the Sunny Bay bus would come to pick up me and Ruby and I was dreading it.

Agatha nudged me. 'I've got something for you.' She handed me a big brown envelope. Inside, I immediately recognised the thick creamy parchment. It was a copy of the *Darkington Times*.

'An early birthday present – your very own copy,' she smiled. 'Yours for life, because you know, once you have a copy, you never need to buy another – unless you recycle it!'

She gave Mum a cheeky wink while I laid the paper out on the table. There was only one story this time. And it had a massive headline:

STORM WITCH AND SON SAVE SIX THOUSAND SPECTRES

'Six thousand?' I said.

Agatha blushed. 'Never let the facts get in the way of a good story, I always say.'

Underneath the headline was the story of Screaming Sands. Our story. Every last detail. It was a rollicking good read. But it wasn't the story that really grabbed my attention. It was the advert underneath:

BACK IN BUSINESS!
Come to Screaming Sands,
the ghastliest ghost town in the world.
Howling gales and torrential
rain guaranteed!
Dark caves, spooky attics and horribly
haunted houses available for hire.
For Halloween bookings contact Davie Hart
at the Poisoned Kettle café, Brine Street,
Screaming Sands, (near Middle Spit Sands).

Just then the sugar bowl started to shake, gently at first, then more violently, until suddenly it flipped up, scattering the sugar granules wildly across the table where they whirled and swirled in wiggly patterns.

'Look!' I breathed.

Gradually the granules were merging together to make a message . . .

WOULD LIKE TO BOOK A ROOM. ARRIVING ALL HALLOWS EVE. FOND REGARDS, DARKLY SAGE, ESQUIRE. P.S. SAVE SOME SNOW FOR ME!

'It looks like I'm going to be busy,' said Mum with a wink.

'It looks like we're all going to be busy,' smiled Dad.

I didn't say anything. I just got up from the table and headed for the kitchen.

'Would anyone care for a Doris?' I grinned.

'I would,' beamed Ruby, her cherry plaits bobbing. 'But don't forget the mermaid cream!'

As if!

Available Now!

Coming June 2013

To find out more about *Screaming Sands*
as well as discover other exciting books, visit:

www.catnippublishing.co.uk